Castle Combe, England.

I **KNOW** *that a lot of villages claim to be the prettiest in England, but I believe that Castle Combe truly is. When I was courting, my husband and I used to take runs t............ always said that we would live the.................... and circumstances meant that we.................... village of my dreams, but one thi....................y with me for ever. On a run there ....ped the question and we went home from Castle C...........*

Your lovely cover brought that memory back to me, clear as a bell, yet it took place over fifty years ago!

— *Mrs T.M., Nottingham.*

£6.99

People's Friend Annual

Dear Reader,

WELCOME to "The People's Friend" Annual for 2011! We have twenty-one brand-new stories from your favourite writers, chosen specially for you. We've also picked out ten of our most popular J. Campbell Kerr cover paintings and let you, the reader, tell us exactly why you loved them so much!

Join us as we look back at children's classic books and see how many of them you remember — and which ones were your favourites! If you're a poetry fan, you can't miss our "Poems For Life" — a selection of poems celebrating the changing of the seasons and special times of year.

Speaking of times of year, make sure that you remember to buy your copy of "The People's Friend" each week. After all, it's your magazine and we simply couldn't do it without you!

The Editor

Complete Stories

p10

J. Campbell Kerr Paintings

p53

2011 Contents

p116

Children's Classics

Poems For Life

p56

Dates For My Diary

*D*O not open until Jan 1, 2011.

The instructions written on the label in my sister Jackie's bold handwriting make me smile. My big sister has been bossing me around all my life. She used to tell me what to play or wear when we were little, but in the last year, she's focused her bossing on getting me to start living again.

I'm so grateful she did.

Now it's January 1, I can open the parcel without feeling guilty that I haven't stuck to her instructions. If I'd opened it early, I'm sure I would have imagined a cry of disappointment over my shoulder.

Not that she could see me, really. Jackie's thousands of miles away in California — living her California dream, we always joke. But I wouldn't have felt right going against what she'd wanted me to do — because Jackie never does anything without a good reason.

But now the time has come to open it.

Peeling back the blue tissue-paper, I unwrap a blue, cloth-bound book, covered in a pretty pattern of tiny red flowers. Opening the front cover, I see it's a diary. A sudden bubble of emotion rises up and fills my chest, making me gasp as tears prickle my eyes. Jackie gave me a diary last year — it helped me pick myself up again and gave me back my life.

I turn to the first page of this new diary and read Jackie's handwriting in the space for today's date.

Go back and read through last year's diary. When you've finished, read the message on the inside of the back cover.

I flick to the back of the diary and there's a small sealed envelope stuck inside the cover. As I read the words written on the front of the envelope, I can't help laughing out loud.

Don't cheat, Panda. Read the old diary first — or it won't make sense.

by Kate Jackson.

Illustration by
Mike Heslop.

7

I feel like I'm six years old again and Jackie's caught me up to some mischief. She still calls me Panda — her version of my name, Amanda. She couldn't say it as a two-year-old when I was born and she's called me it ever since.

So I'd better do as she says, and read last year's first. It's in the drawer of my bedside cabinet — I put it there after I wrote my last entry in last night.

I SETTLE myself down on my bed and lean back against some propped-up pillows, holding last year's diary in my hands. Looking at it now, I remember how I'd felt when I'd unwrapped the pretty green cloth-bound book so delicately patterned with tiny blue flowers, and had wondered why Jackie had sent it to me.

I'd never been a diary sort of person. Writing down what I'd done each day or even thoughts or feelings was never for me. And especially then, at such a difficult time in my life.

I was struggling enough just to get through the days. If I'm honest, I was living like a robot, going about the day, doing the basic necessities of life — shopping for food, the laundry, the cleaning — just enough to keep things ticking over.

Sleep was my friend. At least when it came, I was out of my misery and, if I was lucky, my dreams took me where I longed to be — back with Simon. But when I woke up the reality would hit me. Simon was gone. We should have had years together. But I'd lost him far too young . . .

I was on my own.

Until Jackie sent me the diary. It was somehow as if a little bit of her was there with me. She hadn't sent it for me to write in. The beauty of the diary was that Jackie had already done it for me. She'd written in two or sometimes three things for each week throughout the entire year. Not thoughts or feelings, but, in true Jackie style, instructions for things she wanted me to do.

Now, one year on, I open the old diary at the beginning and read again my sister's first entry written in January the first's slot.

Dear Panda,

I know you're probably thinking why on earth I've sent you a diary — but it's here to give you a regular nudge from me. Turning into a new year without Simon won't be easy for you, so I've made a few suggestions — OK, then, instructions — for things for you to do each week. Nothing too hard, don't worry. But Panda, do try them out and see what happens.

Love, Jackie.

I remember how I'd flicked through the diary to see just what sort of things Jackie wanted me to try.

Put on your wellies and go and jump in some puddles or mud or both.

Feed some ducks.

Go to the cinema in the afternoon.

Cook a new recipe and share with a friend.
Lie on your back and watch the clouds.

The diary was filled with things to do. Nothing drastic, just small things. Fun things. Things to make me look around again and make me laugh. It must have taken her ages to think of enough for the whole year.

So I'd followed Jackie's instructions. I'd felt strange at first, but little by little I felt like I was coming back. I was getting out and doing things again — not just the basics any more. I still missed Simon. I always will. But by following Jackie's instructions, I was starting to enjoy the little things in life again. I felt that I was joining in with life, not just existing on the edges.

And that's what Simon would have wanted.

As I read my way through last year's diary I notice how, after the first few months, I started to add to some of Jackie's instructions. Things like *must do this again* or *loved it*. Gradually I'd added more each time and somehow I'd changed into a diary writer, ending with last night's final entry.

And now this morning I have a brand-new diary. What Jackie wants me to do this year I'm not sure — the answer lies in the secret envelope.

SLIPPING open the sealed flap, I take out a pale blue card covered with Jackie's writing and start to read.

Well, Panda,

What a difference a year makes! I know I can safely say that because of our weekly chats on the phone. I'm so glad you've found your joy in life again.

So now I can stop bossing you around so much, eh? You may have already noticed that I've only written one instruction in this new diary . . .

I hadn't even looked as I'd been so curious about the envelope at the back. I stop reading and quickly flick through the diary. Its pages are still pristine, just waiting for someone to write on them. But not Jackie this year. I finish reading the card.

You don't need me to fill in your diary any more — you can do that for yourself.

Love, Jackie.

Her words make me smile. Jackie's final instruction is for me to do it myself. She's bossed me when I needed it and now she's stepping back.

I can do it myself now.

One year on and I feel so different. My life has changed. I'm enjoying it again and I know filling in dates for this new diary won't be a problem for me. I'll make sure I include plenty of fun stuff, too. There's nothing like jumping in puddles on a rainy day to put a spark into life! ■

THERE I was, on my knees, finishing off the bathroom floor, when George came up behind me on silent soles.

"You've missed a bit," he said.

I got such a fright, I cracked my head on the underside of the basin.

"Go away and find something useful to do," I snapped at him.

That was the trouble, really. I had been retired for a couple of years from my part-time job and had plenty to do, even after fulfilling unavoidable domestic chores. George had been free for only a few weeks and was at a complete loose end. He had no proper plans, and domestic drudgery didn't attract him at all — no surprises there!

Fortunately we were coming into gardening season, which brought plenty of garden chores that, with a little female diplomacy, could be made to look

Life Cycle

by Joyce Begg.

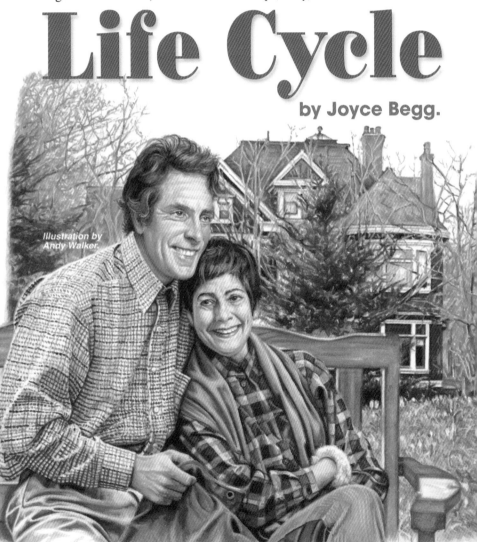

Illustration by
Andy Walker.

like manly projects.

"You could get a greenhouse," I suggested. "They come in kits from the garden centre, or you might find one in the classified ads. You find all sorts of things there; you might well find a greenhouse at half-price."

"Why would I want a greenhouse?"

"Why not? You might really enjoy raising seedlings and onion sets and . . . things."

"I don't think so, Norma. You've really got to know what you're doing with greenhouses — and you have to get folk to look after your plants when you're away."

"Are we going away?"

He shrugged.

"Possibly . . . probably . . . some time."

I sighed and went off to bake a cake for the weekend. Clearly, George's heart wasn't in gardening, which was a pity, because he needed the exercise. He did cut the grass, but everything else was low-maintenance. According to George, all that was ever needed was an occasional stab round the shrubs with a hoe.

T HE mention of going away set George's mind off on another track. "The thing is," he said, "I thought that when we retired we would be able to do more things together. Day trips, long walks and that kind of thing."

"I'm all for that," I said enthusiastically. "Especially if there's a pub lunch at the end." Personally, I thought a long walk might be something that we would work up to, but George leaped ahead on to something more ambitious. It was only a few days later he came in from town full of excitement. As I thought he had only been at the library, I was a little taken aback. There can't be that many thrills in the biography section!

"I've ordered something special for us, but you'll have to come and see it for yourself."

"I see," I said, though I didn't. If it was a holiday, he usually did that on the computer, with me at his elbow making sure that he didn't book us a fortnight in Outer Mongolia.

"You can come now, if you like," he said.

I was intrigued, and put away the vacuum cleaner on the spot.

Twenty minutes later, we were outside the bicycle shop.

"Crikey, don't tell me you've bought yourself a bike!"

"It's not actually paid for yet, but yes, I've had two set aside."

"George, I haven't been on a bike since the kids were learning — and that was in 1976."

"I thought you liked a challenge."

"For you, dear, not for me."

"Don't be defeatist. I thought you'd be thrilled . . . this is something we can do together."

He was right about that, but this was beyond a long walk. This might just be a wheel too far.

"Come on," he said. "Just have a look at them. Gary's put them in the back shop."

I WONDERED how long he had spent in there to be on such good terms with the salesman. I didn't have long to wait to find out. A young man with a very short haircut waved from the far end of the shop, and came across to meet us.

"You've brought her, then, George," he said, reaching out his hand to me. "You must be Norma. Your husband has told me all about you."

Gary — identified clearly by his name badge — pumped my hand up and down with sporty enthusiasm. I smiled weakly, and wondered at this modern tendency to first name familiarity on an acquaintance lasting less than three seconds. Whatever happened to Mrs Parker?

The bikes in question were fetched and wheeled into the front shop by Gary and another assistant — this one's name badge identified him as Jonas.

"Here we are, Norma." Gary showed off the bicycle as if he'd made it himself. "George thought that you'd like this one but, of course, you are free to choose something else if you would prefer it."

We tried them out for size. My bike had nice fat tyres, and a place for a shopping basket. George's was much racier, with thin tyres and a seat so high his nose brushed the handlebar. That was when I realised that we were getting this all wrong.

"Exactly where were you thinking of us going with these bikes, George? I mean, mine would be fine for nipping out for the paper and milk, and I'm sure Sir Chris Hoy would think yours is just the ticket, but what are we actually going to use them for?"

George looked nonplussed, but Gary was quick off the mark.

"You're so right, Norma. They don't really match each other, do they? If you want to go out in the country together, then this might be more what you are looking for."

He gave the bicycles to Jonas, and led us to the selection of mountain bikes. My eyes lit upon a lovely little purple number, chunky yet cute, with eighteen gears. I couldn't imagine when I would use them all, but I was game to try.

12

Children's Classics

"The Secret Garden"
by Frances Hodgson Burnett.

THE SECRET GARDEN" was first published in its entirety as a novel in 1911, having begun life in serial format in the autumn of 1910. It tells the story of the orphaned Mary, sent back from India to England to live with her only remaining relative, a reclusive uncle. She then rediscovers the secret walled garden within the grounds of his house. In bringing the garden back to life, she also brings new vitality to her invalid cousin, Colin.

All of the action in the book centres round the garden, which has been locked since Mary's aunt died many years ago.

The Secret Garden
Frances Hodgson Burnett

Burnett's fictitious garden is thought to have been inspired by the garden at Great Maytham Hall in Kent, and the author's own views on the healing powers inherent in living things come through clearly throughout the story.

Upon initial publication, "The Secret Garden" was not nearly as popular as Burnett's earlier works, including "Little Lord Fauntleroy", had been, and this continued right up till past the author's death in 1924. Its prominence today, one hundred years after its initial publication, is most likely due to the rise of academic and scholarly work relating to children's literature in the late twentieth century. ■

George looked wistfully over his shoulder at the racing model, while Gary wheeled forward a bright red machine that would not look out of place in the Himalayas.

George was seduced immediately.

We were encouraged to try them out in the yard at the back of the shop — under Jonas's eagle eye, of course, in case we careered into a wall and damaged the merchandise. This was a wise precaution. We were both ludicrously out of practice. However, once we had selected our colour-coordinated helmets, we were all set.

Gary offered to have the bicycles delivered the next day and we went home in a glow of achievement and anticipation.

GEORGE would have set off for the Cairngorms first thing the next morning after the bikes were delivered, but I was unwilling to tackle real mountains without a bit of a build-up.

"Why don't we try the park first?"

"The park? You mean two laps of the boating pond and a circuit of the swings? I don't think so. I'm sure we can do better than that."

"Well, I'm not. I want to get the feel of the bike somewhere relatively safe. As it is, we're probably going to put several toddlers at risk. Come on, George, be sensible."

So, the next morning, the pair of us set off, fully accoutred, in the direction of the park. As we left, Margo from next door saw us from her driveway, her eyebrows going up in astonishment.

"Don't ask," I called as George launched himself along a temporarily pedestrian-free pavement. "It's all about togetherness."

Margo grinned.

"Better not let him get too far ahead, then. And, I must say, the colour suits you."

"Thank you. I may need you to roll some bandages later."

I could still hear Margo chortling as I caught up with George.

After two or three early morning sessions in the park, we progressed to the towpath and the corporation cycle track, so in no time at all we were ready for the real thing. Well, George was. I was still a bit apprehensive about "proper" hills.

"Don't be a wimp," he said. "You'll be fine. This is exactly what we got the bikes for, isn't it? Conquering the great outdoors? C'mon, it'll do you good. I'm off to see if Gary's got one of those contrivances to attach the bikes to the car — then it's Snowdon, here we come."

He was talking with his customary exaggeration, of course, but while I was thinking of gentle rolling countryside with occasional pubs, he was thinking rugged. I wasn't sure I could cope with rugged. Something in between would suit me. Our nearest country park was twenty miles away, but that would be a sensible place for our next outing.

WE had to wait a few days because of the rain, which had George pacing up and down the kitchen, stopping only to look out of the window at the sodden lawn.

"You could paint the spare room while you're waiting," I said, putting another load into the washing-machine. "Or you could sort out the loft. You've been talking about that for long enough."

"You have to be in the right mood for jobs like that," he said.

"Do you, indeed. Well, I'm afraid the kitchen floor won't wait for me to be in an appropriate frame of mind. If you could shift yourself from the sink, I'll fill the bucket. Why don't you go and check the cricket score?"

After another two days of rain, I was at the end of my tether. However, before I lost the plot completely, Thursday dawned bright and dry, and we were ready to set off at ten o'clock, the bikes tied firmly to the back of the car. Margo emerged from her driveway at the same time, on her way to a shift in the library. She lowered her car window and called across.

"Got your first-aid kit?" she asked.

"Naturally," I replied gravely. "And a full set of splints."

She giggled.

"There's a good book out on cycling in the Pyrenees. Shall I put it aside for you?"

"Maybe not this week." I smiled.

A gap appeared in the traffic, and she edged her car forward.

"Enjoy your day, folks!"

We did enjoy it — at the start. The weather was warm and bright and lifted the heart. We even found ourselves singing the kind of songs we used to sing with the children when they got bored on long journeys. We passed a lemonade lorry, causing the driver to clutch his steering wheel in surprise as the sound of "Ten Green Bottles" floated through his open window.

"This is the stuff," George said, breathing deeply as we hit the country air. "This is what retirement is all about."

The park was lovely, the conifers tall and brooding, the hardwoods bursting into bright green leaf. And when the countryside opened out, there were fields and moorland, and spectacular views. There were also miles of paths for walkers, cyclists and people on horseback.

"You'll probably find it tough to start with," George said.

"I was OK on the towpath," I replied slightly defensively. "My legs hardly hurt at all."

"This is different. This is much harder going, and you're probably not that fit, so just take your time. I'll try to stay back for you."

I refrained from pointing out that running up and down the stairs a thousand times a day was pretty good for one's general physique. But, for all I knew, he could be right. I could be completely outclassed from the beginning.

Although it was a lovely day, the rain had made the ground muddy. I found myself searching for the driest way through, though George just forged ahead, not fazed at all by the adverse conditions. I kept well back, not wishing to be splattered from what flew off his rear wheel. He glanced back now and then to make sure I was still on the horizon, before charging on. I could see him swerving occasionally, but he managed to correct himself, and seemed to be enjoying the challenge. I was actually quite proud of him.

GEORGE waited for me at the rise, and as I caught up, I could see that exhilaration was taking its toll. He was pink and sweaty.

"Brilliant, isn't it?" he said rather breathlessly.

I agreed with him. I was enjoying the experience far more than I had thought I would.

"It's good," I said. "I must have used every single gear. You look a bit puffed, though, George. I hope you're pacing yourself."

"I'm fine," he said. "This is just healthy exercise."

"OK, but why don't we take a break? I could do with some water myself."

So we had a short breather while his colour returned to normal and he stopped snorting like a dragon.

"At least the next bit's downhill," I said. "Though it looks even muddier."

"It's all a question of technique. You've got to approach these muddy patches properly or you'll lose control."

I promised to take it steady, and off we went.

There is an attraction about travelling downhill at speed that is almost irresistible, and I could see that George had caught the bug. I half expected him to take his feet off the pedals, stick out his legs and yell "Wheee!" What he did do was approach the patch of mud far too fast.

The bike swerved and went off in an easterly direction into a clump of heather, while George went west and landed in a rolling heap. To my shame, my first thought was for the bike. We would have trouble selling it if it was bent.

George was totally winded and lying in a very peculiar position.

"I think I've broken something. Lots of things, actually," he whimpered.

I laid my bike carefully on the grass.

"Have you? Where does it hurt?"

"My body. My body hurts."

"Can't you be more specific?"

"No."

"Shall I phone for help? I have to tell you, they won't get an ambulance up here."

"I might need a helicopter."

"I see. Let's inspect the damage first, shall we?"

To cut a long story short, his injuries totalled one sprained ankle, a jarred shoulder and a bruised ego. It took us some time to walk back to base, with him supporting himself on the mercifully undamaged bicycle, while I brought up the rear in respectful sympathy.

It also took me some time to reattach the bicycles to the car, but I did it while George levered himself into the passenger seat. From there, it was straight to X-ray, a forty-minute wait and confirmation that nothing was actually broken, though a tubular bandage was recommended for the ankle. Altogether, an exciting day.

I T was Margo who saw the item in the cycles column of the classified ads, right next to the greenhouses. She came round to our house for some enlightenment.

"It says here," she read, "*Two mountain bikes, one lady's, purple, one gent's, red, eighteen gears; pensioners' mistake.* That has to be you and George! What happened? Are you both OK? Did you have an accident?"

"We're absolutely fine," I said brightly. "George came off the bike and hurt his ankle, but the swelling's going down now."

"So you're giving up?"

I nodded.

"I'd rather go walking, to be honest, and George has decided that cycling's not for him. He's going to trace his family tree instead."

Margo winced.

"There might be some hidden dangers there, too. Though probably not physical ones. Does that mean I can pack away the rolled bandages?"

I smiled.

"Yip . . . Unless you and Tom are thinking of taking up cycling."

Margo raised her brows.

"You know, that's not a bad idea at all. Don't accept any offers for the bikes until I've consulted the oracle, but I bet he'll say yes."

I grinned delightedly.

"Done deal!" I said. "They couldn't go to a better home." ■

A Grand Night In

G RANDMA, what are we going to do?" Chloe's little face
crumpled as if she was about to burst into tears.
"Why? What on earth is the matter?"
Chloe pointed at the blank television screen.
"Oh, Chloe, don't worry. It's gone to sleep for a while."
Immediately her face brightened.
"Sleep?"
"Yes, that's all, it will wake up again in the morning."

by Mary Cookson.

*Illustration by
Gerard Fay.*

17

At that moment, Hal rushed into the room.

"Grandma, why won't anything work?"

For the first time in two years our grandchildren were staying with us for the weekend. My daughter Caroline and her family had been living in Switzerland. Now they were home again and it was wonderful to see how the children had grown.

I had been planning this special weekend for months. But, as it happened, it was threatening to be one of the stormiest spells of weather of the year. I knew from past experience that if there was a power cut, it could be at least twelve or more hours before the power would be reconnected. It happened maybe once a year and we were used to it and coped with the inconvenience.

"We've had a power cut, Hal. I'm afraid it might be tomorrow morning before it comes back on again."

I was not prepared for the stricken look on his face.

"But I was in the middle of a game on the computer." His voice sounded shocked.

Our old computer didn't really live up to Hal's modern model that he was used to at home, but as I'd planned a whole weekend of outdoor activities, I'd thought it wouldn't matter. How wrong I was. This could turn into a siege.

"I knew Dad should have let me bring the laptop," Hal said.

"But that wouldn't have worked here."

"Oh, Grandma." He groaned. "You don't need electricity."

"Oh, I see."

"Grandma?" Chloe was tugging at my skirt. "Can I watch 'Shrek'?"

"No, darling."

Immediately she ran off and returned with the DVD in her hands.

"The DVD won't play without electricity," I said.

"Because it's asleep?"

I nodded, trying not to see the disappointment on her face. This was not going to be easy.

HAL was looking around as if he had discovered a totally new world. "What shall we do, then, Grandma?"

"We could go for a short walk, before it gets dark," I said lamely.

Outside, although it wasn't pelting down with rain, it was certainly looking like it might at any moment, and the usually beautiful distant hills were shrouded in mist. It was just past four o'clock and a little late on a winter's day to be setting out on an expedition, even if it hadn't been very, very windy.

Both sets of eyes were turned to me expectantly.

"You've brought your books with you," I said. "How about just settling down by the fire and reading? Or we've plenty of jigsaws?"

"Will you read to me?" Chloe said, clapping her hands delightedly.

"Yes."

Hal grimaced, then wandered off. Even though I couldn't see what he was doing, I guessed that he was trying to make a miracle happen. I heard the faint click as light switches were turned on and off. It was tempting to shout to him to leave them alone, but I knew that at ten years old and a bright boy, he wouldn't get up to too much mischief — not yet, anyway.

But I was beginning to worry about how to keep two lively youngsters entertained for a whole evening. Caroline had warned me that Chloe was happy as long as she could watch her favourite DVD.

"It's a ritual at the moment. I ration it to a quarter of an hour, so that it spreads out, but you know what kids are like, they get something into their heads, and have to do it. I've tried giving her another DVD instead, but no, it must be 'Shrek'."

So what should I do? The story would entertain Chloe for a time, but what about Hal? If only we could have gone outside and played ball. But that was out of the question. My half-hearted suggestion of a walk was one thing, but now the wind was gathering speed and battering noisily at the roof. I could tell that we were in for a stormy night, in more ways than one.

CHLOE was enjoying the story, snuggling down and clutching her favourite doll, and suddenly I realised that she was falling asleep. Half-past four in the afternoon was not a good time for a three-and-a-half-year-old to take a nap.

Quietly, I closed the book.

Chloe opened her eyes and blinked.

"Come on, Chloe, we have work to do."

I took hold of her hand. At the bottom of the stairs we paused.

"Hal, will you go and gather up all the candlesticks you can find and bring them here, please?"

"What?"

"Anything that holds a candle."

Suddenly he disappeared.

"Me, me," Chloe said.

"Here, Chloe, you can take the candles out of this tin."

It was my candle tin, really an old chocolate biscuit tin, which held a quantity of new and used candles. Phil, my husband, always laughed at me for buying candles.

"We could light a church with what you've got stashed away."

"Just in case," I'd say, but of course, when it was just the two of us, we only needed a few candles for an emergency. However, this was different; I had two young children to entertain and a dark house to make light.

"Grandma, oh, lovely, pretty colours, and . . ." Chloe wrinkled up her nose. "Smells funny."

I laughed.

"Yes, it's candle and beeswax, but they'll make the house all bright and cheerful."

Finally, Hal returned with ten assorted candlesticks and tea light holders.

"Wonderful," I said, and he half smiled.

"Now, we'll put tea lights in the hall so that it is safe. But Chloe and you, Hal, must be careful." I put on my gravest face and stared at each of them in turn. "Candles can be dangerous."

Chloe, her eyes wide, nodded.

"Do you understand?"

"Yes, Grandma," they said in unison.

"And you, Hal, as the oldest, you must take special care that Chloe keeps away from the candles."

"Yes, Grandma."

He took hold of Chloe's hand and knelt down.

"Chloe, you must do as I tell you," he said seriously.

"Now, do you know what we're going to do?" I said, finally satisfied that everything was out of harm's way.

Two solemn faces turned to me.

"We're going to make a pie."

"You can't," Hal said, a look of triumph on his face.

"Why not?" I asked innocently.

"No electricity."

"Ah, but we don't need it."

SILENTLY I offered a prayer to whatever it was that had stopped me from discarding the wood-burning stove in the old scullery, which had since become part of the extended kitchen. I had bought a new electric cooker, but even so, I still couldn't bear to part with the range.

"I've been slow cooking our evening meal in it all day. It burns wood to keep the house nice and warm and it has an oven. We'll just check how it's getting on."

As I opened the door, a wonderful warm meaty smell wafted towards us.

"Our casserole; cooking it for so long makes it tender. Just in time for when your grandpa gets home. So this is where we'll cook the pie."

"What sort of pie?" Hal was not going to give in easily. "I don't like plums or raspberries. I'm bored. Wish I was at home, then I could see my friends."

"We'll have an apple pie. But I'll need your help, Hal, because Chloe and I can't do all the work."

"When will the electricity come on? Why do you live here, Grandma?"

"Because we love it here, Hal, and your mum loved it as well. Even when she was as small as you, Chloe, she helped me with the baking. She just loved getting her hands all floury and then drawing pictures on the table. But her greatest treat was when we made cakes and she licked the bowl."

The Royal Mile, Edinburgh, Scotland.

*Y*OUR *illustration of the Royal Mile in Edinburgh must have been drawn on the day I was last there. Normally, every time I go through to Edinburgh, it is raining or very grey and dull. However, I really had my eyes opened last summer when I went through to visit a friend and found the entire city centre bathed in brilliant sunshine. Princes Street Gardens were filled with people, all of them relaxing and enjoying themselves.*

It didn't take long for my friend and I to abandon our planned day of shopping and join the other people just making the most of the sunshine. I've never spent such a great day in Edinburgh and I'm sorry for thinking that it only ever rained there!

— Mrs A.C., Dundee.

J. CAMPBELL KERR.

"I'm going upstairs." Hal stomped out of the kitchen.

Chloe gazed after him.

"Come on, we'll make a lovely pie," I said.

"I want Hal to help."

"I know, Chloe. He'll be back, I promise."

I wasn't so sure. The evening seemed to stretch ahead of us and I had no idea how to keep Hal happy. He had left his new iPod at home, so he couldn't even listen to some music. To me, the silence of the house was relaxing, but I knew that it was different for a child.

In the end, it didn't take long for Hal to reappear. Chloe and I made a lot of noise rattling the scales and tapping measuring spoons and laughing and giggling. Hal edged back into the kitchen, trying to look as if he didn't care what we were doing.

Chloe was covered in flour and making little pictures on the work surface.

"Can I mix it?" Hal said, as if he couldn't wait any longer.

"Why, of course, Hal."

Steadily, he mixed the butter with the flour until it was fine breadcrumbs.

"That's perfect. Where did you learn to do that?"

"I like cooking. Sometimes Mum lets me help."

"That's wonderful. I bet if you offered to make something for your mum, she would love it."

Once the pastry had been turned out on to the floured board, it was time for Chloe to help to roll it out and place the thinly sliced apple in the middle.

"We're making a rough pie. Fold in the pastry over the top and make a crusty edge then sprinkle sugar on top."

"Sprinkly. Sprinkly little star."

Hal laughed.

"That's not it, silly."

"Oh, yes, when you're baking a pie, you should always sprinkle a few stars into it," I said, winking at Hal.

"Chloe, do some more sprinkly," Hal said seriously.

Chloe sprinkled sugar on the pie.

"Now a dusting of cinnamon and then into the oven," I said.

The time had flown by and it took me by surprise when Phil came into the kitchen.

"What a glorious smell! Pie and casserole. What a combination."

"We did it, Grandpa," Hal said proudly. "We made the pie."

"And me," Chloe piped up.

"What a feast we'll have," Phil said.

After a candlelight supper, Hal asked, "What shall we do now?" He gazed wistfully at the television in the corner.

"Bathtime for Chloe, then you, Hal, and afterwards we could play a game."

"It's too dark. I play on the computer before bed," Hal said. "I wish Dad had let me bring the laptop, but he said I wouldn't need it." He frowned.

I glanced at Phil, who gave a tiny shrug.

"Come on, Hal, we'll take the kitchen torch and go into the garage and find some lanterns. Must have some more torches somewhere; we'll need them for getting you two to bed. Chloe still needs a light for the night."

"She's such a baby," Hal said.

With a little more persuasion, he reluctantly accompanied his grandfather to the garage and they were gone for an hour.

"Grandpa's found a load of stuff, and I'm going to help him clear the garage out tomorrow. He says if I find anything I like I can take it," Hal said, when they returned carrying a couple of large torches and a lantern.

Chloe and I were sitting by a roaring log fire and I was drying her hair with a towel.

"I'm going to have plaits," Chloe said proudly. "Lots and lots of plaits."

"And because it's a special occasion, I'm sure your mum won't mind if you stay up a bit later, so that we can have a game of snakes and ladders."

"Snakes and ladders. That's a rubbish game," Hal said.

"Pretend it's one of your computer games," Phil said.

Hal groaned.

"Yeah, right."

Our grandson really was grown up at times. I realised that it was still a long time until bedtime.

"Well, it's that or read a book or do a jigsaw."

Hal shrugged.

"Suppose so," he said without any enthusiasm.

IT was with a heavy heart that I set out the small card table. How was a game of snakes and ladders going to keep a lively ten-year-old interested for more than a few minutes?

Phil had brought down a pile of games from the loft and when Hal looked through them, he had shown no interest at all. True, they were all from when Caroline was young, but still, I thought something might have caught his eye.

I remembered him as a baby and then a toddler and then an eight-year-old who was always excited at staying with us for the weekend. But, I thought, times change. We haven't seen each other for two years and he's growing up, it's only natural.

In the end, it was Hal who became really competitive about the game and punched the air when he won. His eyes were bright and he smiled in the way that I remembered from those other times when he had stayed with us.

"That was fun," Phil said.

"It was OK," Hal said casually.

I tried to hide my smile. It felt just like when Caroline had been a little girl and we had turned off the lights and played all the games by firelight — Scrabble, Monopoly, Connect Four.

"Right, cocoa and a story before bed."

Chloe sat between us, her eyes shining, her golden plaits hanging down over her shoulders.

"I'm off; I'm not listening to an old story. Can I have the big torch, Grandpa, so that I can read in bed?" Hal trudged off upstairs.

"Don't you want any cocoa?" I called after him.

"No, I don't like it."

T HE rain had begun spattering against the window-panes and outside darkness clung to the house. It was noisy, with the thudding of branches against the glass and a howling wind that broke over the roof like a wave and then subsided.

But inside, the living-room was warm and cosy. The firelight glinted on the ceiling and the furniture. Sparks crackled and flew up into the air and every time they did, Chloe took a great breath and said, "Look, Grandpa!" then sipped her chocolatey drink.

Candlelight flickered on our

Children's Classics

"The Water Babies
(A Fairy Tale For A Land Baby)"
by the Rev. Charles Kingsley.

T HIS children's novel by the Rev. Charles Kingsley started life as a weekly serial in a magazine, appearing in 1862-63, before first being published in its entirety in 1863.

The story centres round Tom, a young chimney sweep, and is a moral fable of the kind so popular in the Victorian era. There is, however, an interesting underlying satire in parts, especially those challenging the scientists of the day and their closed-minded approach to new scientific advances. This likely stems from Charles Kingsley being a great advocate of Charles Darwin and, despite his strong Christian faith, a supporter of Darwin's ideas on evolution. In fact, in 1859, three years before the first instalment of "The Water Babies",

faces. With the big torch on the coffee table beside the sofa, there was just enough light for me to read a chapter from "Alice's Adventures In Wonderland".

Finally, Hal crept into the room and sat down on the rug before the fire and picked up the mug of cocoa that had been left there for him. He listened attentively to the story as he munched on a biscuit.

Phil carried Chloe to bed and we tucked her in. The beam from the large torch on the landing cast a glowing light into her bedroom.

"Tell me a story, Grandma," she said sleepily.

I sat down on the floor beside her bed, held her hand and began to tell a

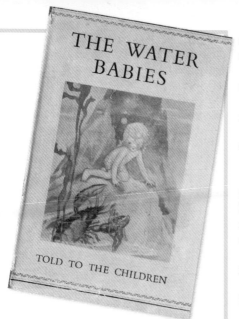

THE WATER BABIES

TOLD TO THE CHILDREN

Darwin sent Kingsley an advance copy of "On The Origin Of Species", which Kingsley was quick — and one of the first — to praise.

"The Water Babies" was extremely popular upon publication and right through until the 1920s, though changing tastes in children's literature since then have seen its popularity decrease slightly. "The Water Babies" has been the basis for several stage adaptations and also a popular animated film made in 1978, and the book remains a fondly remembered part of many childhoods. ▪

story of a white rabbit and soon she drifted off to sleep.

Downstairs, Hal was stretched out on the floor.

"Well, it's been a grand night in," Phil said.

"What does that mean, Grandpa?"

We laughed.

"It means, my lad, that it's been fun doing things together, like baking and playing games and reading and nearly all of it by candlelight."

Hal was thoughtful for a moment.

"Do you think the electric will be off the next time we come?"

"No, it'll be fine, it's only because of this very high wind," I said, trying to reassure him.

Suddenly, with a sinking heart, it occurred to me that he might tell his mum that he didn't want to stay with us again. Why hadn't I been prepared for bad weather? All the plans I had made were because I was still thinking of Hal as an eight-year-old who loved to scramble up the hillside. Of course, he was now used to beautiful mountains in Switzerland.

My plan for lots of walking and coming home to a wonderful evening meal was no longer as exciting as it used to be when he was younger. Hal had forgotten about the times when the electricity had been cut off when he visited. Chloe had been quite happy, because for her it had been an adventure.

"Only, I wondered if I could help you make some cakes again? And Chloe as well. She'd love to lick the bowl, wouldn't she, Grandma?"

"I'm sure she would. And we can do that even if the electricity is on," I said, overjoyed to see again the Hal that I loved and knew so well.

"Can we? Great. That would be cool."

"Yes," I said, "that would be cool." ▪

S ARAH had one last look in the mirror, her hands trembling slightly as she tucked her hair back behind her ears. She straightened the collar of her crisp white shirt and sighed, feeling uncomfortable and slightly ridiculous in the smart new navy suit she'd saved up and bought for the occasion.

"I feel like an air hostess," she muttered to herself as she slammed the front door behind her.

Practising Breathing

by Sheila Norton.

Illustration by Mike Heslop.

It had all been so much easier at college: so much less hassle in the mornings. She'd got used to lying in bed until the last minute, and then rushing to class in jeans, T-shirts and trainers like all the other students.

Now, trotting to the bus stop in her high heels and pencil skirt, she wondered, for the twentieth time since the alarm clock had woken her that morning, whether she'd done the right thing in choosing an office job. Why hadn't she gone for evening work at the local vet's, like her friend Karen? She could have lain in bed until teatime every day!

A bleep from her phone interrupted her thoughts just as her bus arrived.

She fumbled in her shiny black leather handbag, feeling cross and flustered as she dropped the phone, then her purse, as she tried to find the right money to pay the bus driver.

Why had she bought this stupid, useless pint-sized bag? What was wrong with the lovely, practical, pink canvas rucksack she had carried her college books around in? Anyone would think she was trying to be someone she wasn't: someone stylish and self-assured, and used to going to work in a smart city office!

FINALLY settling down in a seat at the back of the bus, she read the text message from Natalie.

Good luck for your first day! Don't be nervous! Knock 'em dead! XX

Don't be nervous — huh! But Sarah smiled as she put the phone back in her bag. It was nice to know that Natalie was rooting for her, and she'd be able to phone her tonight and tell her all about it. They could have a giggle together like they always did, and everything would feel all right.

Sarah fidgeted in her seat, straightening the navy pencil skirt and watching from the window as the suburban houses gradually gave way to blocks of flats and office buildings on the outskirts of the city.

Not far now.

She tried to practise deep breathing to calm her nerves, and an image of Natalie came unbidden to her mind. Natalie lying on her back on Sarah's lounge carpet the previous Thursday when she'd come over for the evening — her long brown hair spread around her face like a veil, her eyes closed, her hands folded loosely over the mound of her abdomen.

"I have to breathe," she had said cheerfully.

"Well, I should hope so!" Sarah had retorted, and they'd both laughed.

"I have to practise breathing like this," Natalie had persisted, demonstrating. "And count — slowly — one . . . two . . ."

"Very clever!" Sarah teased. "What are you trying to do — teach the baby maths before he's even born?"

"If he's listening! But I think he'll be too busy finding his way out of here."

"Are you looking forward to it, Nat?" Sarah asked. "Being a mum? Staying at home, just you and the baby, for the first year, instead of going out to work?"

"I think I'll be working hard enough!" Natalie replied, sitting up quickly and looking shocked. "Being a mum is a career in itself!"

Right now, getting off the bus in the city centre and heading for the building where she would spend every day working in the office of an insurance company, Sarah suddenly felt a sharp pang of envy. Lucky old Natalie!

How Sarah would love to be cocooned in her own home, too, painting the nursery and practising breathing exercises instead of putting herself through the torture of this first day at work!

BEING the new girl wasn't something she particularly minded. It hadn't been all that long since she was a new girl at college, after all — but then, she'd been one of a whole crowd of new girls, and the first term had been so much fun, with all of them getting to know each other.

But it was different now; everyone else would know each other. Everyone except her would know what they were supposed to be doing. She'd feel lonely, and stupid, and scared. Give it a couple of hours and she'd probably be wishing she was back at college!

Sarah walked into the office where she'd had her successful interview a month earlier, and paused in the doorway, looking around, hoping to see a friendly face.

Everyone looked up, and for just one frightening moment nobody smiled, nobody spoke, and Sarah thought seriously about turning on her heels and running straight back out of the building, jumping on the next bus home, going back to bed and pulling the duvet over her head.

"Hi!" a man at the desk next to the window eventually said. He got up and walked towards her with his hand stretched out and, finally smiling, shook her hand and led her towards the desk next to his.

"I'm Rob — you must be Sarah. I'm afraid you'll be working with me! This'll be your desk and your computer. But I'm sure you'll want to hang up your

coat and stuff first . . ."

"Come with me, Sarah!" A woman of about thirty, whose desk faced her own, laughed. "Honestly, men are useless! Never mind your desk and your computer for a minute — I'll show you where the important things are.

"The ladies', the tea and coffee, and the water cooler! I'm Jenny. If you need to know anything, ask me — don't bother asking Rob!"

Rob grinned as Sarah followed Jenny back out of the door on a tour of the facilities.

"Don't be too long!" he called after them. "It's going to take me most of the morning to impart all my worldly wisdom about the job to Sarah!"

"Only one morning," Jenny commented dryly. "He's all right," she added to Sarah in an undertone. "Just don't get him started on Pink Floyd or Led Zeppelin!"

"I won't," Sarah promised, wondering what would happen if she did, but already glad of the banter.

But she realised, as she carried a plastic cup of water back to her desk ready to start learning the basics of her new job, that her heart had stopped thumping quite so painfully and her hands had stopped shaking. This was going to be all right. It *had* to be all right. It was going to be her life from now on, and she had to get used to it.

She sat down, straightened her shoulders and took a deep breath as she turned on the computer in front of her.

"Right," Rob said, sliding across the floor to her desk on his swivel chair. "First things first. Let's get you logged on to the system as a new user. Want to choose yourself a password?"

THE morning flew past at a rate of knots, and before she knew it, Jenny was asking her if she wanted to go out and grab a sandwich for lunch. "That'd be really nice, thanks!"

Sarah was so grateful that Jenny was being friendly. She'd been worried about the age difference. Everyone else was so much more confident and experienced than her. All the exams, all the merits and certificates in the world couldn't make up for that.

"I can't believe how well you've done today!" Jenny exclaimed as they walked to the sandwich bar along the street. "The HR department told us you've only just finished at college. Have you worked with computers before?"

"No. This is my first job," Sarah admitted. "And to be honest I've got a thumping headache from concentrating on everything Rob's been showing me!"

"Well, he's impressed — and so am I. You're a quick learner and I'm sure you'll fit right in!"

"Thanks!" Sarah smiled to herself as they queued together at the sandwich bar. Now all she had to do was last out the day without collapsing in a heap or doing anything stupid, and they might even decide to keep her on!

*　　*　　*　　*

"Well? How did it go?"

Natalie was on the phone almost as soon as Sarah got through the front door.

"Oh, my. That was awful!"

"Oh, dear. That bad?"

"No, no, not the job. I'm talking about the journey home in these shoes! I'm not wearing them tomorrow. It'll be the old comfortable ones —"

"But how did it go? Come on, I'm going to burst if you don't tell me in a minute!"

"Oh!" Sarah laughed. "Don't do that! Don't you go bursting — not for another six weeks, if you can help it!"

SHE threw herself down on the sofa, holding the phone with one hand and rubbing her sore feet with the other.

"The job was OK." She felt herself smile. "In fact, it was better than OK! D'you know what? I think it went really well! I think I'm going to enjoy it! And they actually seemed to think I did all right! Isn't that amazing?"

"Of course it's not amazing! Why should it be amazing? Look how brilliantly you did at college — passing all your exams with flying colours!"

"Yes, but that was different! Now I've got to do everything properly, because I'm being paid!" She savoured the sound of this. Being paid! At last, after all these years, she was going to be a working woman, doing a proper, paid job in an office.

"And about time, too, Mum," Natalie said seriously. "You've deserved to be paid for the last twenty years, as far as I'm concerned — all those years you gave up to look after us, and helping out in the classroom for nothing. And you know how proud we all are of you, passing business studies and computer exams at your age . . ."

"All right, all right — enough about the age, if you don't mind! It's bad enough that I'm working for people not much older than you!" Sarah laughed.

This morning she'd been envying her daughter — leaving her job to stay at home on maternity leave. But why? Hadn't she already been there, and done that? Now it was her turn to move into the next chapter of her life. New girl? Ha! Why, she was almost a grandmother! As if there was anything these bright young things in her office could do that she couldn't learn how to do just as well!

Yes, it might be scary but, like Natalie, she just had to practise breathing! ■

Kinsale, County Cork, Ireland.

*M*Y *husband and I had the most wonderful holiday in Kinsale many years ago. This picturesque resort is one of the most popular on the south-west coast of Ireland and we had nothing but sunshine the whole time we were there.*

I'm a real history buff and loved the star-shaped fortresses built in the 17th century, guarding the harbour. I went on a guided tour of Charles Fort and was lucky enough to visit St Multose Church, built in the 13th century and still in use today.

I also discovered while I was there that the Lusitania *was sunk just off Kinsale in 1915 with a loss of over 1,500 lives — it was a sad moment on an otherwise very happy holiday.*

*— **Mrs M.K., Manchester.***

J. CAMPBELL KERR.

On The Wings

by Christina Jones.

"TOMORROW is the birds' wedding day," Granny Large said as she fastened my balaclava, a dreamy, faraway look in her eye. "All the little birdies in the world find their one true love on Valentine's Day and they get married. Isn't that romantic, Tina?"

"Greugh," I agreed. "Shnurph . . ."

I didn't have a speech impediment, I hasten to add, it was just that Granny Large had fastened my balaclava to the top buttons of my liberty bodice, anchoring my chin to my chest and thus restricting my airway.

It was a chilly February morning in the late 1950s, and our prefab was strangely quiet. Just me and Granny Large and the dog, who had been titivated by my mother the night before and was now wearing a party hat at a rakish angle. Tinsel adorned his collar.

Granny Large wasn't good at dressing children, but as I was incapable of doing it myself, my dad was away, and my mother and Granny Small had rushed off early to catch the bus into town, there wasn't much choice.

Granny Large smiled distantly as she threaded my mittens-on-elastic through the sleeves of my gabardine raincoat.

"The first man you see on Valentine's Day will be your one true love. The one you'll marry. I'm going to make sure I see my photo of Russ Conway the minute I open my eyes. Russ Conway is my one true love. Isn't that wonderful, Tina?"

"Murmph nith boolsh . . ."

I flapped my hands a bit. There seemed to be an awful lot of one true loves, but I had other things to worry about. I'd got two mittens on one side and a lot of elastic on the other.

"You must never sign Valentine's cards. They have to be secret."

Granny Large shoved my feet into my wellingtons. Wrong wellingtons, wrong feet.

"Secret *billets-doux* to and from your one true love. Oh, I do love Valentine's Day, don't you, Tina?"

"Kormph . . ."

"Wonderful." Granny Large patted me smartly on the head.

"Now off you run to school. You'll be able to tell Mrs Filkins all about Valentine's Day, won't you?"

I nodded as much as my constrictions would allow and hobbled away from our prefab towards the Mixed Infants. Mrs Filkins, our teacher, would be really impressed with the depth of my knowledge. I'd be able to put my hand up in class and answer all the questions. I had insider information.

Of Love

Illustration by
Patricia Ludlow.

Despite the wellington
boot problem, I skipped
happily across the
playground, just as the bell
was ringing.

Sadly, uneven asphalt and
wrong-footed wellingtons
are not a good combination. I
came a proper purler just in
front of the veranda steps.

The rest of the Mixed Infants, who were lined up straight with
their fingers on their lips, howled with laughter. I just howled.

"In the name of all that's holy." Mrs Filkins hauled me to my feet and
looked at me. "Who dressed you this morning?"

"Granny Large did, miss!" Cousin Gillian broke ranks, waving her hand
above her head.

"She must've because she's the only one left at the prefab because Tina's

33

mummy and Granny Small have gone into town today. They caught the early bus. They had to be there by nine o'clock."

My knees hurt but I bravely sniffed back my tears. Because of the balaclava-liberty bodice connection they got stuck in my throat. I tried to cough and couldn't. Panic set in and I flapped my truncated arms a bit. I knew my mother and Granny Small had gone on a Very Important Mission, one that little girls mustn't ask about.

"Betcha don't know where they are, do yer?" Cousin Gillian sneered.

"Murmphlett," I muttered just before catching a glimpse of my knees and bursting into proper tears.

I attempted to add that my mother and Granny Small had gone somewhere secret, but failed.

"I knows where they've gorn," Gillian continued, preening smugly.

"You don't."

The Mixed Infants sniggered. I couldn't see why my mother and grandmother going into town on a Very Important Secret Mission was funny. In fact, being pretty sure that my wellingtons were filling with blood, I failed to find anything funny at all.

"Ah." Mrs Filkins nodded, right-footing my wellingtons and not seeming to notice that I was standing in a puddle as she did so. Then she briskly rubbed my knees, smearing gore and grit into the grazes.

"Of course. It's Tuesday. Were they all dressed up, Tina?"

"Phrlup-hic-manchly . . ." I sobbed, nodding.

Mrs Filkins snapped my balaclava away from my liberty bodice.

"There. Better?"

"Yes, thank you." I sniffed. I was a polite child. "But my feet are wet and my knees hurt."

"Never mind. You'll live." Mrs Filkins clapped her hands.

"Now get into line — and children, who can tell me what tomorrow is? The first person who can tell me what tomorrow is can be Milk Monitor all day."

For the first time in living memory I knew the answer. I tried so hard to shoot my hand into the air but sadly, owing to the mis-threaded mittens, I only managed to get my hands to elbow level.

"Miss! Miss!" Gillian's eyes glowed with demonic fervour. "Miss! It's Valentine's Day, miss!"

"Clever girl, Gillian." Mrs Filkins smiled one of her toothy grins that made her look like the wolf in "Red Riding Hood".

"Boys and girls, Gillian is going to be Milk Monitor. Now, let's all file into school and get ready for assembly. This afternoon after story time, we'll talk about Valentine's Day."

Mrs Filkins blew a shrill blast on her whistle, and I was slightly mollified as we shuffled forward through the intermittent drizzle. I knew loads and loads about Valentine's Day.

Thanks to Granny Large I'd probably be made Wet Playtime Monitor for the whole week, which meant giving out the comics and Plasticine. I'd make sure Cousin Gillian got all the comics with the last pages of the stories missing and got only the grey Plasticine.

I was still smiling to myself when Mrs Filkins blew her whistle again. We all concertina'd to a halt.

"Who — and the person who can tell me this can be Wet Playtime Monitor all week — can tell me what today is?"

I frowned. Today? To be Wet Playtime Monitor? Oh, no! That wasn't fair!

I looked at the puckered brows. No-one else seemed to know, either. I began to relax, my vision of retribution on Cousin Gillian beginning to re-emerge.

"Let me give you a clue." Mrs Filkins raised her voice above the keening wind.

"It's Tuesday and it involves Tina's mother and Granny Small catching the early bus and being all dressed up in their best clothes . . ."

Everyone except me shot their hands into the air.

"Miss!" Gillian kicked my smarting knees, making me wince.

"Yes, Gillian."

"It's court day, Miss! Tina's daddy's in court!"

Everyone laughed. Except me.

"Well done, Gillian!" Mrs Filkins beamed.

"You're going to be a busy little girl today, aren't you? Two monitor jobs. Well done. Anyway . . . in we go, children. In we go . . ."

I SPENT the whole of assembly in a state of confusion — even more than usual. If my mother and Granny Small had gone to see my dad, then how come Mrs Filkins and the Mixed Infants and Cousin Gillian knew and I didn't?

What was a court day? Maybe, I thought, sucking my thumb through "Jesus Wants Me For A Sunbeam", it was something to do with jesters. Court jesters — yes! That must be it! My dad was really funny. He'd be appearing in front of someone royal — like pretty Princess Margaret — dressed up in red and yellow and a funny hat with bells on, doing his jester act.

I supposed it was only for grown-ups and that's why it was a secret and why I hadn't been told. Having sorted that out, I beamed with relief as we chanted our way through the prayer that always scared me into sleeplessness, the one about if you don't wake up in the morning you hope your soul will be kept by the angels — mainly because I'd seen pictures of angels in my scripture book and I didn't like the look of them at all.

They looked like Mrs Bledlow's big boy Jerome, only in a frock. I didn't want them keeping any part of me, thank you very much.

Sadly, it was all downhill from there. Cousin Gillian became very prissy over the dual monitor roles and it was me who got the torn comics and the grey Plasticine at playtime. I also got the bottle of milk with the top pecked off and bits floating in it.

Still, I thought, once we got through the tedium of storytime — Mrs Filkins had a particularly monotonous reading voice and sometimes she fell asleep in the middle of "Billy Goats Gruff" — I'd be able to impart my Valentine's Day knowledge. And maybe, just maybe, I'd be made Cloakroom Monitor. We all liked being Cloakroom Monitor because it meant you could try on everyone else's coats and eat the sweets in their pockets.

Today's story was "Goldilocks". Mrs Filkins managed to stay awake until the baby bear made his appearance. Fortunately we all knew how it ended, so we did colouring-in until she woke up again.

The Call Of Spring

T *HE blackbird pipes a tune on crystal thorn,*
And ponders on which season's song to sing!
No sign of green, midst snow-entangled morn,
No inspiration for the call of spring.
Pert robin hops hopeful for a crumb or two
In traced design on frosted window-sill.

R IGHT, children!" Mrs Filkins gave a little snort and tried to look as though she'd been awake all the time, like my mother does when she's "just resting her eyes".

"The End! Now, who's going to tell me about tomorrow? What's tomorrow, children?"

"Valentine's Day!" we chorused.

"Who's going to tell me about Valentine's Day?"

Hands waved, chests were thrust forward.

"Um . . ." Mrs Filkins scanned the faces.

"All right, Tina . . ."

"The birds get married, miss," I said in a rush, Granny Large's words repeating in my head.

36

His scarlet bib a cheerful, crested hue,
A "thank you" chirp from grateful beak does spill.
The starlings scold a-chatter in the trees,
And idle snowflakes crowd in aimless way.
How long will nature tantalise and tease?
How long will winter overstep her stay?

— *Elizabeth Gozney.*

Willie Shand.

"They wear white dresses and carry flowers and go to church like my auntie Sylvie nearly did, and the vicar says words and then they're married and they live in little birdie houses. And —" I took another huge gulp of air in case anyone dared to interrupt me. I could see Cloakroom Monitor looming large.

"An' the first man you sees tomorrer morning is your one true love. So even if it's the postman or the milkman or your dad, it don't matter — that's the man you'll marry."

I looked around triumphantly, not quite sure why everyone was rocking with laughter. Maybe they were amused at learning something new. I sucked in more air.

"An' — an' that's not all. Your one true love sends secret billy-doos, miss!"

Exhausted, I sat down, and beamed round the classroom.

Cousin Gillian and Lesley Turner were sprawling across their desks, helpless with mirth. Everyone else was chuckling.

Mrs Filkins hiccupped before managing to control herself.

"Lovely, Tina . . . if a touch inaccurate. Some rural myths in there that seem to have got . . . er . . . a little muddled, but at least you tried. Now let's see if anyone else knows anything about Valentine's Day?"

Lesley Turner did. With Cousin Gillian nodding and encouraging her by repeating every word, she tripped out the biggest load of rubbish I'd ever heard. Nothing at all like Granny Large had said — all stuff to do with fourteenth-century aristocrats in France and Chaucer and Samuel Pepys and ancient love rituals. She never as much as touched on sparrows in tulle frocks or marrying the postman or billy-doos.

"Gertcha!" I spluttered. "That's all piffle."

"Actually . . ." Mrs Filkins did her big-teeth thing. "It's far from piffle, Tina. I'm very impressed. Lesley's extra-curricular after-school tuition is clearly paying off. Lesley can be Cloakroom Monitor."

"That ain't fair!" I was practically exploding with indignation. "She'm only being Cloakroom Monitor because 'er mum's a school guvnor! She just said some ol' history book stuff. An' Gillian just copied 'er! It ain't true. None of it ain't true."

"Tina, you mustn't be rude to Lesley or Gillian. You can come and stand beside me for the rest of the afternoon with your hands on your head and you won't get a go in the sweetie jar."

Everyone laughed. A lot. Cousin Gillian especially. And she took two sweeties out of the jar and waved them in front of my eyes while I smouldered with anger.

I WAS still smouldering when the bell went and Mrs Filkins belted off for a Woodbine behind the coal bunkers. My knees still hurt and my arms ached from the hands-on-head thing, and there wasn't anyone to make sure my wellingtons were on the right feet.

Lesley Turner and Cousin Gillian and some other girls all called Linda were giggling in the cloakroom about the Valentine cards they were going to get in the morning. Apparently they were all sending cards to Craig Allcock in Miss Payne's Big Class because he looked a bit like Billy Fury.

I concentrated on my wellingtons. As I had no idea who Billy Fury was and as Craig Allcock had greasy hair, boils and compulsory adenoids I doubted if Billy Fury would be delighted with the comparison.

"Are cards the same as billy-doos?" I queried, my tongue protruding from the corner of my mouth as I changed feet again.

"Billy-doos? Billy-doos?" Lesley Turner's fat face wobbled in derision.

"You're mad, you are. Mad and stupid. And you've got your wellingtons on the wrong feet."

I sat on the cold concrete floor and tried again.

Cousin Gillian sneered as she sauntered past me, arm-in-arm with the Lindas.

"We'll show you our Valentine cards in the morning. We'll get proper cards — not silly billy-doos — and you won't get nothing!"

All giggling, they ran off across the playground leaving me alone in the cloakroom.

By the time I'd hobbled back to the prefab, my feet hurt as much as my knees, but neither of them hurt quite as much as my feelings.

Granny Large and the dog — minus his party hat and tinsel but with telltale sparkly bits round his mouth — were still the only ones at home. Maybe my dad's court jester act had gone into extra time.

Munching my way through Granny Large's tea of condensed milk and banana sandwiches as she plinketty-plonked air-piano to Russ Conway's greatest hits, I told her about Lesley Turner and Cousin Gillian's silly notions about Valentine's Day, and how they were sending cards to Craig Allcock and how they'd never heard of the birds getting married or billy-doos and how they'd all laughed at me.

Granny Large stopped plinketty-plonking and looked at me. She shook her head. Then she smiled.

"You mustn't worry your head about silly girls like them," she said, straightening the limp lace at her throat.

"I know how to deal with them. And no, best you don't ask questions. You've got more'n enough to cope with. You just hang on here while I nip out to the corner shop for a moment . . ."

THE next morning the prefab was awash with lopsided bunting. My mother, a vision in burnt-orange, lime and fuchsia, had arrived home somewhat unsteadily ever so late the night before. She'd fallen over in the living-room while high-kicking and singing "What Shall We Do With The Drunken Sailor?" with my dad on one side of her, and Granny Small, wearing a deerstalker and smoking a cigar, on the other.

I'd peeped out of my bedroom door then smiled happily as I snuggled back into bed, pulling the eiderdown up to my chin. My dad's court jester act must have gone down really well.

"A bit of a celebration last night," Granny Large said, gesturing to the bunting and the balloons.

"Your daddy's a free man again. And no-one else is awake yet so I've made your breakfast then I'll get you dressed . . ."

I smiled sleepily at the pretty balloons, and at the dog who was wearing the deerstalker, then I sat obediently at the table to plough my way through a breakfast of sugar sandwiches and toast and dripping all on the same plate.

"Now," Granny Large said as she thrust me, still munching, into the full school regalia — this time with no mistakes at all — "you know what today is, don't you?"

I puckered my brow and screwed my eyes up tight and thought and thought and thought. Then I beamed.

"Valentine's Day."

"Good girl. You remember what I told you about Valentine's Day, don't you?"

I nodded.

"Well, if you look out of the window you'll see the little birdies all getting ready for their wedding day," Granny Large said.

"Go on — look . . ."

I looked. An entire avian wedding celebration — complete with small brown birds wearing veils and top hats — was taking place on the window-sill.

I clapped my hands with delight, sadly splattering dripping across the dog.

"Are they real?"

"Of course they're real."

"They look a bit — um — stiff . . ."

"Wedding nerves."

I nodded — of course. If Granny Large said they were real then they must be. Grown-ups never told fibs. So, if the birdie bride and groom and attendants looked a little bit like the papier-mâché robins we had on the Christmas tree, I must be imagining it.

She'd been right and Cousin Gillian and Lesley Turner had been wrong. It was the birds' wedding day!

T HE postman's been," Granny Large went on.

"It was all right as I'd already feasted my eyes on darling Russ Conway at first light — and he's left you all these *billets-doux* . . ."

I blinked at the pile of envelopes in her hand.

"For me?"

"For you. Open them, Tina . . ."

I did. It was like my birthday only a little bit more confusing because none of the cards were signed. They were very pretty though, all pink hearts and flowers, and they all said that someone loved me very much . . .

I blinked again and wrestled the envelopes away from the dog, who was chomping his way through them with a blissful expression.

I grinned happily. They all had my name on the front, all in different handwriting in different colours . . .

"They're real billy-doos, aren't they?"

"They are, presh." Granny Large nodded as she glanced out of the prefab window.

"Now, if you hurry up I'll get you to school on time. Come on, quickly, quickly . . ."

With the cards clutched in my hand and Granny Large shoving me from behind, I hurtled out of the front door just as a group of Miss Payne's Big Boys, led by Craig Allcock, passed the prefab.

"Go on!" Granny Large hissed. "Say hello and happy Valentine's Day to Craig."

"Happy Valentine's Day, Craig," I parroted obediently.

"Yer what?" Craig sniffed. "Oh, yer — right. 'Appy Valentine's Day back, Tina."

"There!" Granny Large beamed at me. "He's your Valentine. Your one true love! Now, let's get you to school . . ."

We scampered into the playground at a brisk pace just behind Craig and his cronies. Lesley Turner, Cousin Gillian and the simpering Lindas were all in a huddle by the coal bunkers and they leaped out on Craig en masse.

"Gertcha!" Craig cried in fright as they all pressed cards into his hands. "Wotcha doin'?"

"You're our Valentine." Gillian preened and primped and looked coy.

Lesley Turner did the same, only more wobbly. The Lindas just went pink and giggled.

"I think you'll find," Granny Large said in her loudest, poshest voice, "that you're too late. Craig doesn't need your *billets-doux*. Tina and Craig have already exchanged Valentine's Day greetings. Craig is Tina's one true love.

"Isn't that right, Craig?" she went on firmly.

"Er — yerss." Craig nodded, shoving the cards back into Cousin Gillian's clenched hands while eyeing Granny Large warily.

"Me an' Tina 'ave said 'appy Valentine's ages ago."

Lesley Turner's fat lips wobbled and her puffy eyes blinked. The Lindas just burst into tears.

"We saw the birds getting married, too, didn't we, Tina?" Granny Large towered over Cousin Gillian in a threatening manner.

"Both of us. And I'm a grown-up and I don't tell fibs. We saw the wedding, didn't we, Tina?"

I nodded, smiling happily.

"How many *billets-doux* did you get?" Granny Large continued. "None? Oh, dear . . . Tina had dozens. Show them, Tina . . ."

I thrust the mass of pastel beribboned and beflowered and be-hearted billy-doos under their noses.

"Noooo!" Cousin Gillian screamed again.

"Yes!" Granny Large nodded.

"Now, all you nasty little girls say sorry to Tina for doubting her and laughing at her, while I just go and have a word with Mrs Filkins about the reallocating of the monitors' duties . . ."

As she swept regally up the veranda steps, and Cousin Gillian and Lesley Turner and the Lindas all muttered apologies, Craig Allcock — adenoids and all — grinned at me in a soppy manner.

I grinned back happily. It was simply the best Valentine's Day a girl could wish for . . .

41

Caught In The Act

WE simply have to go shopping on Saturday afternoon, Will. It's our last chance to get you something half-decent to wear before the wedding, and I need to look round for a new bag to match up with my navy blue suede shoes," Joan said.

"But it's the bowls play-off on Saturday afternoon between Sid and me. I couldn't possibly miss it," Will protested.

Joan pretended she hadn't heard.

"Our Carol says she'll drive us to the new Merrybrook Shopping Centre in her car. You really do need a new suit for your granddaughter's wedding, Will."

"Can't we go in the morning instead?" Will pleaded.

"No, we can't. Carol's working on Saturday morning. You've been putting this off for weeks now and it's our last chance to go." Joan was beginning to get irritated. "The world will not come to a sudden end if you don't play bowls with Sidney Colclough."

"You don't understand the importance of this play-off, Joan. If I don't turn up Sid will claim the game by default. That means he'll go into the team. No, this is a crucial matter — I can't go shopping. We'll go on the train one day during the week, I promise you that.

"Anyway, I don't know what you're making such a big fuss about. I've got a perfectly good suit in the wardrobe upstairs."

"I can't go next week, Will, her wedding's next Saturday! I've so much to do I can't think straight, and that old suit of yours hasn't seen daylight since our Carol's wedding twenty-two years ago."

Joan could feel her temper rising, but, being the wise woman she was, she deliberately made herself calm down. She knew she'd never get Will to the shopping centre if she lost her temper. Years of experience had taught her that her husband could be led but never driven.

"Besides, Will, I hate to say this but you've put on a bit of weight since our Carol's wedding and much as it suits you, I really don't think you'll fit into that suit. You know you need a new one, love," she coaxed, adding a warm smile for good measure.

Then she patted Will's rounded stomach gently.

"My teddy bear, that's what you are!"

Will looked pleased but wasn't giving up.

"Joan, this is vital. It's the only way the rest can decide which of us is playing in the championship. No, I just can't miss it."

I'll have to change tack; I'm losing this argument, Joan thought cannily. So she said nothing further — for the moment.

"At least go and try it on, love — just to make sure you can get into it," she said.

WILL muttered and mumbled but finally clumped upstairs to inspect the suit. Joan could hear the bang as the wardrobe door was pulled back, the clang as the hangers smacked together, then the loud sound of puffing and panting as he tried to squeeze his surplus flesh into tight trousers. She smiled to herself.

They really did need to go shopping. A new suit for Will was essential, but making sure she bought the little navy suede clutch bag she'd remembered from her last visit was, too. The one she and Carol had decided on last time was just too big and overwhelmed her strawberry pink outfit, she'd decided. No, that particular little navy blue bag would be just right with her navy suede shoes.

She went upstairs and perched on the end of the bed.

by Sheila Culshaw.

Illustration by
L. Antico.

43

"Those trousers are far too small, Will, aren't they?" she said, her arms folded.

"No, not if we move the buttons a bit," Will persisted, but he was purple in the face from the effort of holding his breath.

"You look like Mr Pickwick and I am not going to my granddaughter's wedding with you dressed like that. It's all nonsense you having to go tomorrow. I really cannot see why the pair of you are so worried about who's playing in a silly old bowls team, anyway."

She glared at Will, then looked at him again and burst out laughing. He looked so funny.

"Oh, what am I going to do with you, love? Nobody could ever accuse you of spending a fortune on clothes, could they? Come on, come shopping with me," she wheedled.

Will finally agreed he would go. He had no choice. But he decided he'd not tell Sid about the change of plan until he'd thought up a convincing alibi for not going.

After their evening meal — when Joan had made Will his favourite, steak and kidney pie — the telephone started to ring.

"Would you answer that for me, Will, love? It's probably nothing much and my hands are all wet from the washing-up."

Will picked up the receiver.

"Hello, is that Will?"

"Yes."

"It's Daphne here. Oh, I am glad I've managed to catch you, love. Sid's not at all well. I think he's coming down with the flu or something and he's just gone up to bed. He says he's sorry but he'll not be able to meet you tomorrow, so you'll have to play in the team. He's really very upset about it, but he says an agreement's an agreement and he wants to stick to it."

"Oh, I am sorry, Daphne. Never mind the match, you tell Sid to take it easy. Make him drink a tot of whisky with some hot water in it and a teaspoon of

Children's Classics

"Anne Of Green Gables" by L.M. Montgomery.

FIRST published in 1908, "Anne Of Green Gables" was intended to be fiction for all ages, and since publication has sold more than fifty million copies worldwide.

The story of orphan Anne Shirley, mistakenly sent to a couple who had requested a boy, and how she gets on in life once the couple decide to keep her, entranced readers, as did the setting of Prince Edward Island, Canada, drawn from the author's own childhood experiences.

The book was so popular that demand for sequels was high. The first, "Anne Of Avonlea", was published in 1909, only a year after the original book, and the final one, "The Blythes Are Quoted", was

Anne of Green Gables

L. M. MONTGOMERY

completed by the author shortly before her death in 1942.

A prequel, "Before Green Gables", written by Budge Wilson, with authorisation from the heirs of Lucy Maud Montgomery, was published in 2008.

Each year, hundreds of thousands of fans of Anne-with-an-E make their way to Cavendish in the Prince Edward Island National Park, to see the setting which inspired such an important and fondly remembered piece of literature and to learn more about both the fictional characters and L.M. Montgomery herself. ∎

sugar. That was always my old mam's cure for a cold. It'll sweat whatever's wrong out of him."

He tried very hard to sound sympathetic as he ended the call.

"Thanks for letting me know, Daphne. Tell Sid I'll phone him tomorrow night to see how he is and that Joan sends her love."

Then he put the phone down and sauntered through into the kitchen, rubbing his hands as he went.

"Seems that poor Sid's got the flu, so we'll be all right for going shopping tomorrow afternoon after all," he said.

Joan smiled, patted his arm and promised he could watch the football as soon as they got back.

AT two o'clock the following afternoon, the loud, high-pitched toot from Carol's car announced her arrival. They drove the few miles to the out-of-town shopping centre. Joan and her daughter were soon talking excitedly about wedding arrangements and Lucy and John's honeymoon in Bermuda. Will sat quietly and miserably in the back seat. He hated shopping centres.

After an hour of looking round several menswear outlets, Will was finally persuaded that a grey suit with a soft pinstripe really looked smart and that he needed two new white shirts. He also conceded that the tie with a slight hint of strawberry pink was the perfect co-ordinating colour to go with Joan's wedding outfit.

He even half-smiled as he admired himself in the full-length mirror.

"No, not bad; not bad at all, is it?" he said, viewing himself from all angles.

Both women and the young salesman agreed effusively.

"Right then, that's the suit bought, but you definitely need some new shoes, Dad," Carol said, looking pointedly down at the well-creased pair Will always wore. But Joan insisted on buying the navy blue suede clutch bag before they carried on shopping.

It was in the shoe shop that Will came face to face with Sid. There he was, head down, trying to get his feet into a pair of black lace-up shoes. He looked a bit red in the face, Will noted. Joan and Carol stood to one side. Daphne looked at Joan.

"Well, that was a short illness, lad — glad to see you've made such a speedy recovery. I thought last night you were at death's door. It must have been my mam's old whisky remedy that did the trick."

"What on earth are you talking about?" Sid asked in genuine confusion. "I've not been ill. Daphne told me last night that you were the one who was poorly, that's why I'm here."

Both men turned as one and stared hard at Daphne, who had moved over to stand next to Joan and Carol. Both elderly women looked guilty, but Joan's daughter looked completely mystified.

"Well, it seems to me that there's definitely been something going on here, Will," Sid said, looking pointedly at his wife. Then he turned to the shop assistant. "Thank you, love, this pair will do me very nicely."

The two men walked out of the shop with dignity. Sid carried his shoes. Their wives and Carol followed behind.

"There's nothing to say, is there, Joan? You made this up between the pair of you, didn't you?" Will hissed in Joan's ear. She nodded her head. Daphne was looking contrite, too.

As they walked away from the shops, Sid suddenly brightened up and turned to his pal.

"I think your bowls are still in the back of my car, Will."

Will nodded his head in agreement.

"Well, it seems to me that that patch of grass over there looks as good as any for the play-off. What do you say? Are you with me in this?"

"I am that." Will smiled.

The two elderly men walked to the car park to fetch their bowls bags from Sid's car, leaving their womenfolk behind. Then they climbed over the car park fence on to the square of lawn surrounded by shrubs and perennials. They both inspected the turf with half-closed eyes.

"Yup, it'll be all right," Will agreed.

Joan, Daphne and Carol sighed and went to sit on one of the benches.

"Might have known we wouldn't get away with it," Joan said to Daphne. Daphne nodded back.

"Get away with what?" Carol asked.

Joan explained the situation to her daughter, who immediately burst out laughing. Then all three watched the game that was being earnestly played in front of them.

Will skilfully rolled the jack into a perfect position.

"Now, it's not exactly crown green standard, but your turn now, Sid," he said with dignity.

Carefully, Sid placed his shot. The ball spun slowly up to the jack and stopped.

"Beautiful shot!" Will cried. Then Will knocked the jack with his ball and they were off.

By this time a fair few shoppers, admittedly mostly bored male ones, had stopped to offer advice and encouragement. There was a ripple of applause when Sid was eventually declared the winner of the game.

The two men walked over the grass to smiles and congratulations and pats on the back. They carefully zipped their bowls back into their bags.

"Ready for the off?" Will asked with dignity.

"I'm ready," Sid replied.

I'M glad you're coming to the reception next Saturday night, Daphne," Will said politely as they walked slowly up the hill to the car park.

"Yes, and I'm really glad you're coming, too, Sid," Joan said equally politely to Sid. "Will, love, just have a quick look at what Daphne's bought for the wedding."

Will glanced inside a carrier bag and caught a glimpse of blue.

"Very nice. Yes, very nice indeed," he decreed.

"Well, we did get our own way," Joan said as they followed their men back to the car park. Then she dug her friend in the ribs and they both started giggling.

Carol was watching her determined-looking dad and his friend marching in front of them with their bowls bags swinging at their sides. The women were carrying all the carrier bags.

"Who'd believe this tale if I ever told it to anybody?" she said to her mum.

"Just you make sure you don't — we don't want to be a laughing stock," Daphne and Joan warned.

Carol's face was expressionless but she couldn't help thinking that the four of them were worse than children. Her little Alex was only four and seemed to have more sense!

She grinned amiably at her mum and her dad and their friends when they reached the car park.

"Dad — and Sid — could I ask just one thing? Please don't bring your bowls bags to Lucy's wedding, will you?"

They both shook their heads and laughed loudly at the idea.

"Don't be so silly. There's no need to worry about that, our Carol," her dad said.

Fortunately Carol didn't see the deliberate wink that passed between the two elderly men . . . ■

The Girl In The Daisy Dress

I SAT on the wall and watched the setting sun transform the sea into a glittering expanse of pink and gold. Scarlet geraniums flourished in Grandmamma's bright blue pots, fishermen shared a joke across darkening turquoise waves, sleepy seabirds called to their mates, and the cliffs above the village shimmered under a haze of wild flowers.

It was a beautiful evening, and I wished I could enjoy it.

"She's very pretty, Nikos," Grandmamma said tentatively.

"Who is?"

Grandmamma didn't answer. She leaned over the wall and waved a hand at the young woman walking along the narrow cobbled alley below us.

"Hello, Sophie," she called, using the only English greeting she knew. "Hello!"

The girl heard us and looked up, beaming when she saw Grandmamma. She was wearing a long green dress embroidered with daisies, a wide-brimmed straw hat trimmed with blue ribbons trailing from one hand.

"*Geia sas,*" she called back in Greek, waving her hat and laughing.

Grandmamma was right: she was very pretty. Masses of wavy brown hair framed a lovely heart-shaped face and her eyes were a wonderful hazel. I didn't realise I was staring until she smiled at me, a soft blush spreading over her cheeks as she held my gaze. She waved again, and walked down the alley and up the flight of steps at the end, daisies floating around her ankles.

I watched her go.

Grandmamma let out a huge sigh beside me.

"You won't impress any pretty girls in those scruffy old jeans and T-shirt, Nikos," she said, half-scolding. "And you looked so handsome in uniform: tall and slim like your grandpapa."

"I don't care," I said, but I couldn't stop myself gazing after that ripple of daisies. "I'm not interested in pretty girls any more, Grandmamma."

She put a comforting arm round my shoulders and hugged me, as though I was still her little Nikos and had never moved away to Athens to join the police and fall in love. She and Grandpapa had brought me up: I'd lost both parents when I was three and they had whisked me away from the big city to this tiny fishing village in the southern Peloponnese. Grandpapa was gone now, but Grandmamma hadn't changed one bit. She had just turned eighty-six and seemed more energetic than ever.

Her black dress smelled comfortingly of cooking. She'd been baking batches of her delicious cakes all afternoon for Mrs Lampeti to sell in the local *kafeneio*.

"You can't grieve for ever," she said. "It's been nearly two years now, Nikos."

"I know."

She wasn't going to give up that easily.

"You could at least try talking to Sophie," she said. "I met her in the market the other day and we got chatting — she's very nice and she knows enough Greek to get by, but I'm sure she'd rather talk to someone who speaks good English, like you."

I glimpsed a last tiny flutter of green and was surprised to feel my broken heart flutter in response; then she was gone and the alley started to fill up

by Deborah Tapper.

Illustration by
David McAllister.

with deep purple shadows.

"She's bought that old house on the cliffs," Grandmamma continued. "According to Mrs Lampeti, she wants to do it up and turn it into a nice little guesthouse. She's sorting out all the details herself: there's no sign of a husband or boyfriend helping her." She shot me a quick sidelong look. "I think she's lonely and would enjoy some male company. She's about your age, and I'm sure you'd find you've got lots of things in common if you just tried talking to her . . ."

Old Manos ambled by, leading a drowsy donkey. Cooking smells filled the air: fried fish and crab, herbs and green lentils. I swung my long legs over the wall and stood up.

"Stop matchmaking, Grandmamma," I said. "I'm not ready for it yet."

"I'm doing nothing of the kind."

"You are. You've done your best to marry me off to every woman you can think of since I came back. You even tried to set me up on a date with Mrs Lampeti, and she's ninety if she's a day!"

Grandmamma tutted.

"Don't exaggerate, Nikos."

I really did want to find out more about Sophie, but I felt a sharp stab of guilt. I hadn't even looked at another woman since Eleni.

"She's a sophisticated entrepreneur and I'm just a thirty-year-old ex-policeman who paints pictures for tourists." Dionysios pushed his wet nose into my palm and I reached down, patting the big dog's rough coat.

"But you're a nice boy and Sophie's such a sweet girl — you'd like her, Nikos."

✳   ✳   ✳   ✳

I couldn't sleep. Although I painted outside, I kept my unfinished canvases in the bedroom and the air was thick and sticky with the smells of linseed oil and turpentine. I'd returned last summer, intending to stay with Grandmamma for a few months while I got my life back in order. The painting was meant to be therapeutic, so I was amazed when some tourists asked if they could buy my pictures.

Summer slipped into autumn and I stayed on, helping with the olive harvest and working on the fishing boats during the winter. It was hard work but I flung myself into it, getting home so tired and stiff I could barely pull my clothes off before falling into bed. Now the fishing season was drawing to a close and the first tourists had arrived. I'd sold a good number of paintings to them last year — a steady trickle of visitors found their way to the village — but once a month I'd loaded the finished canvases into my battered old Fiat and driven round the coast to the larger resorts. Often I was gone all week and Grandmamma clucked over me liked a worried hen when I got home.

Moonlight flooded the window, open to catch any breath from the sea. I got up, pulled my jeans on and tiptoed out. Dionysios was curled in a corner of the courtyard. When I opened the door, he rose to his feet, stretched and padded over, wagging his tail. I patted him then swung my legs over the wall and stared at the sluggish moon-tipped wavelets, remembering Eleni.

We couldn't have been more different. She was a city girl: smart, sharp and self-confident. I took her to museums and art galleries and for long romantic walks in the National Gardens. She teased me about my lack of city gloss and dragged me to all the trendiest restaurants. Despite the differences, we fell in love, married and had three wonderful years together.

Until the accident, when my whole world fell apart.

My thoughts drifted back to the stunning girl in the daisy dress and I swung my heels against the wall, feeling horribly guilty. Grandmamma was right — I'd have to smarten myself up or I wouldn't stand a chance with a gorgeous creature like her.

Dionysios put huge paws up on the wall beside me and I dropped an arm around him.

"What do you think?" I asked him, ruffling his fur. "Would Eleni want me to move on?"

The dog barked loudly in reply and Grandmamma flung a window open behind me.

"Is that you, Nikos?" she demanded. "What are you doing out there?"

"Nothing." I looked up, suddenly self-conscious. "Sorry I woke you."

She leaned her elbows on the window-sill, gazing down at me, her shrewd black eyes twinkling in the moonlight.

"Thinking about Sophie?"

I slid off the wall.

"Goodnight, Grandmamma."

I COULDN'T seem to get Sophie out of my mind, so I took a fresh canvas up to the cliff top and settled down to paint the bay, Dionysios snoring at my feet. The sun glittered off the sea, drenching the distant islands in violet haze, and a solitary white fishing boat moved sluggishly across the water. It was very hot and I was struggling to catch the elusive ripple of light on the waves, my face screwed up in concentration and the tip of my tongue poking between my teeth. A cheerful voice called, "*Kalimera*", and I glanced up to see Sophie smiling warmly at me.

"Good morning," I replied in English. "Have you been there long?"

"Only a little while." She looked fresh and lovely standing in her daisy dress amongst the long grass and wild flowers, long curls tied back with a blue ribbon. I was suddenly very conscious of my unruly black hair, paint-spattered T-shirt and the worn old deck shoes I'd thrust my feet into so carelessly that morning.

"Your grandmamma said I'd find you up here. I'm Sophie Grant."

"Nikos Kalkos," I said, putting my brushes down and shaking her outstretched hand. Dionysios opened a lazy eye, yawned and went back to sleep.

"Can I see?" She came to stand beside me, studying the painting. "That's really good!"

"Would you like me to paint something for you?" I offered. "Or maybe you'd like to look through some of my finished canvases? I don't just paint seascapes; there're some landscapes I'm quite proud of." I swallowed hard. A whisper of wind flicked her skirt against my threadbare jeans. She was so close she must have been able to hear my heart thudding.

"You're my first customer this year, so I'll give you a half-price discount on any picture."

That delicious smile widened. Tiny lines crinkled around her eyes and I wanted to kiss her right on the tip of her sweet little turned-up nose.

"That's very kind of you, Mr Kalkos, but I'm not looking for a painting at the moment."

"Call me Nikos — everyone does." I was grinning like an idiot and Dionysios flicked a disdainful ear in my direction. "So what are you looking for?"

"A policeman." She gazed at me with huge hazel eyes and I felt my knees turn to water. "Everyone in the village says you're a detective."

"I was," I said. "I resigned last year."

Her face fell.

"Oh."

"But that doesn't mean I can't help you," I added quickly. "What's wrong?"

"This is going to sound really silly, but . . . I think there's someone hiding in my house!" The words came out in a rush and her cheeks flushed a pretty shade of pink.

"You mean the Ghost House?" I said it without thinking. It was what we'd called it as kids, ever since my fearless best friend Petros Argyros had come running out after a dare, swearing that he'd been chased through the trees by a ghost.

Sophie's smile faded and she looked annoyed.

"That's what the builders call it."

"The Argyros brothers?"

"Do you know them?"

I nodded.

"We were at school together."

"Could you talk to them for me? I didn't think my Greek was that bad, but I'm sure they said they'll only renovate the ground floor because of the ghost, and now I keep hearing noises at night."

"You're staying there alone?" I was annoyed to feel my hair prickle.

Sophie raised her chin and looked at me defiantly.

Goatfell, Arran, Scotland.

ALL it took was one look at your cover and I was back on Arran over forty years ago on a day out with my mum and sister. We took the ferry over from Ardrossan and hired bikes to explore the island, although neither my sister nor I realised at the time that it had been over twenty years since our mother had last been on a bike!

We had a terrific morning and stopped for a picnic on the beach at Brodick. It was a hot summer's day and we were all a bit sleepy after lunch, but it was my mum who was protesting the most about having to get back on her bike.

After touring round the island all afternoon we made our way back to the ferry and handed over the hire bikes. My poor mum could hardly stand up straight when she got off her bike and was bent over double with aching muscles by the time we got home. It took a hot bath and a few days' rest before she fully recovered from our eventful day trip to Arran!

— Mrs M.C., Hamilton.

J. CAMPBELL KERR.

"It's my house," she said, then her lower lip tightened. Her big eyes filled with angry tears and it was all I could do to stop myself from taking her in my arms and kissing her.

"If there is anyone there, I'll find him," I promised, laying a comforting hand on her arm. "But you can't go back until I've got this sorted out. Mrs Lampeti's got a spare room. If I talk to her, I'm sure she'll put you up."

"What about the builders?"

I gave her a confident grin.

"I'll pack my things up and talk to them now."

THE Argyros brothers saw my car pull up outside and were waiting for me when I went in.

"Nikos!" Petros punched my shoulder, grinning broadly. I'm tall but he towered over me, work-hardened muscles bulging beneath his old T-shirt. "Had enough of sitting in the sun all day, painting pretty pictures for the tourists?"

"I helped out on your uncle Theo's boat all winter," I reminded him.

Petros caught sight of Sophie behind me and winked at his two younger brothers, Georgios and Andreas.

"I know — and if you're looking for some more work, there's plenty here."

I grinned back. I couldn't imagine these tanned, broad-shouldered giants being scared of anything, especially not a childhood ghost. Sophie must be mistaken.

"How's the renovation going?"

Petros's teasing grin vanished and his brothers looked uneasy.

"Fine," he said. "We just need to see about getting the water and electricity connected, then we're done."

"You've certainly done a great job on the downstairs rooms," I said, "but what about upstairs?"

"It's the Ghost House," Andreas said in hushed tones.

I shrugged.

"That's just what we called it as kids."

Petros shuffled his feet.

"It's haunted, Nikos."

"You mean you're going to pack up and walk away without finishing the job?" I gazed at them. "That's not like you!"

"We don't want to go," Georgios muttered, glancing at Sophie.

I wondered if this would all turn out to be an elaborate practical joke, but the three brothers looked very serious.

"If I get rid of this ghost, will you finish the renovation?"

"Of course we will!" Petros said. "We'd be happy to."

"That's settled then," I said. "I'll stay here tonight — and every night until I find out what's going on."

"You're going to sleep here?" Georgios shuddered.

I nodded, feeling more determined than ever.

"I'm going to solve this mystery, and if it involves catching a ghost, then I'll do it."

"Better you than me," Andreas muttered.

They went back to work, but as they picked up their tools I overheard Georgios whispering something to his brothers about me being in love with the pretty English girl. I blushed, hoping Sophie hadn't heard it, too.

＊　＊　＊　＊

I brought Dionysios back with me and searched the house after they'd gone, but I didn't find anything. The old place was very sturdy. It wouldn't take the Argyros brothers long to renovate it and turn it into a guesthouse, assuming I could dispose of the ghost first. I explored the upstairs rooms thoroughly, then went back downstairs. There was no point in checking the loft as I didn't have a ladder, and no-one could be hiding in that cramped space under the shallow pitched roof.

Sophie had been staying downstairs. She had left me an inflatable mattress, two oil lamps, a pile of cooking things and a small camping stove in a cool, stone-flagged room that smelled of fresh paint. It was starting to get dark, so I lit the oil lamps then sat down to a supper of fried squid, crusty bread and a huge slice of Grandmamma's cake.

I wasn't intending to sleep, but I must have dozed off because it was pitch black outside when Dionysios woke me with a low growl. I reached for my torch, remembering Petros's tale of a white, shrieking shape that came gliding through the lemon trees towards him.

"Hello?" I got to my feet, flashing the torch around. "Is anyone there?"

"Nikos, it's me."

"Sophie!" It was difficult not to kiss her, especially when she took my hand and smiled at me like that. "What are you doing here? I thought you were with Mrs Lampeti."

"I wanted to make sure you were OK." Her dear face looked even lovelier in the soft light. "And to say thank you for doing this."

"You didn't walk up here?"

She smiled.

"Petros was feeling guilty. He called into the *kafeneio* for a late cup of coffee and offered to run me up in his van."

"He did?" A wave of jealousy swept over me. "Is he still around?"

"He wouldn't stop — but he wished you good luck with the ghost-catching."

I brewed more coffee and we sipped it, Dionysios snoring at our feet.

"Have you heard anything?" she asked.

"Not yet." I searched for something to say. "Grandmamma says you want to turn this place into a guesthouse — is your husband going to help you?"

"My marriage broke up," Sophie said. "I came here for a fresh start."

"I'm sorry."

"I'm getting over him." She looked down and bit her lip. "I heard about your wife," she said softly.

"She was chatting to a friend on her mobile phone and stepped out in front of a car." It hurt to say it out loud, but not as much as I'd been expecting.

"Nikos, I'm so very sorry . . ."

Sophie laid a gentle hand on my arm. "Is that why you came back here?"

I nodded.

Fair Maids

AS pale as a ray
Of winter sun,
As frail as a web
By a spider spun,
Facing the damp
And the wind and the cold,
Fearless and tough
As the brave knights of old,
Audacious but gracious
And destined, perchance,
The fair maids of February
Start the floral dance.

— *Dorothy Morris.*

"My boss Ioannis suggested it. He knew I enjoyed painting. He took me aside before I left and said if I wanted to go back, he could pull a few strings and get me reinstated on the spot."

"Do you think you will?"

"I don't know. I might have been there now if some tourists hadn't seen me painting and asked to buy the picture." I looked up, meeting those lovely hazel eyes. We didn't need to speak, we just leaned towards each other and my lips began to tingle, anticipating the kiss. Then there was an unearthly high-pitched shriek right outside the window and Dionysios leapt up, barking furiously.

Sophie clutched me.

"Nikos, there's something out there — I saw it!"

I LOCKED the doors, searched the ground floor thoroughly then ran upstairs, going from room to room and finding nothing.

"Can you see anything?" Sophie called from the stairs.

"Nothing." I shone the torch over the walls and floor while Dionysios sniffed around, his tail quivering. "Whatever it is, it must be —"

The blood-curdling scream sounded right above me. I could hear something hissing and scuffling around overhead.

"What was that?" Sophie was beside me, listening to the odd sounds coming from the tiny loft space.

"I'm not sure," I said, "but I'm fairly certain it isn't a ghost."

There was an old table in the corner. I dragged it over, positioned it under the loft-hole and climbed up cautiously, pushing the cover aside. If I stood on tiptoe, I could just see into the narrow space under the rafters.

"Nikos!" Sophie flung both arms round my legs as Dionysios bounded up

beside me, making the table wobble dangerously. "Please be careful!"

I shone the torch towards the angry hissing, the beam revealing several pale, spectral shapes . . .

"Oh, wow!" I gasped.

"What is it?" Sophie asked.

"Owls." I grinned down at her anxious face. "A whole family of owls."

"Owls?"

"Barn owls," I confirmed. "There's a mum and five cute little fluffy balls up there. You must have seen their dad flying past the window, hunting for mice. They've probably been using this house as a nesting site for years, ever since Petros and I were kids." Then the funny side of it hit me and I started to laugh. "I can't wait to see his face when I tell him that his ghost has turned out to be an owl!"

THE Argyros brothers took it surprisingly well, especially when I admitted that the owls had given us quite a scare. Petros slapped me on the back and said he wouldn't have stuck his head through that hole for anything, Georgios laughed, and Andreas suggested that Sophie could put a camera up in the nest site and use it as a tourist attraction next year.

Sophie liked the idea when I suggested it over a meal a few weeks later. I sold several paintings, bought myself some smart new clothes, had my hair cut and asked her out. I took her to the cosy *taverna* in the nearest town. We sat under a gnarled fig tree and she told me how the renovations were progressing while we ate stuffed vine leaves and fish baked with vegetables.

"And I thought you could call it the Owl House," I finished.

"It's a brilliant idea," she said, her eyes sparkling. "I love it."

She smiled at me then laid her hand over mine. I felt my heart flip over and over.

"I don't know what I would've done without you, Nikos — you've been wonderful."

"Sophie . . ." I wanted to tell her how much she meant to me and how I couldn't imagine my life without her, but my English deserted me and I could only gaze into her eyes.

"Nikos, I . . ." she began. Then she stopped as though she didn't know what to say either, so I leaned across the table and kissed her very gently under the shade of the fig tree.

And when Sophie smiled and kissed me back, I knew neither of us needed to say anything at all. ■

Parish News

THE Reverend Martin Stratton went into his study and, from the pile of papers on his desk, found the sermon he'd finished writing the night before. He took a quick glance through his typewritten notes and decided, for the umpteenth time, that he really would have to think about buying a computer.

And yet, his ancient typewriter still worked . . . more or less! Admittedly, one or two of the keys tended to stick and the "Q" no longer printed but, with a certain ingenuity, he could usually find alternative words to those containing the letter "Q".

He smiled to himself, remembering how "Quinquagesima Sunday" always posed a problem, but his faithful old typewriter could still manage "the Sunday Before Lent" instead, so perhaps the new computer could wait a little longer.

"I'm off now, dear," he called to his wife from the hall. "I'll see you in church."

"Have you remembered your glasses?" Pauline called back from the kitchen, clearing up from breakfast.

He went back into his study and, after some searching, found them.

"I've remembered them now!" he called to Pauline, with a chuckle.

Walking across the gravelled driveway to the church there was a chill in the air, but the clear blue sky promised another lovely spring day.

"Morning, Vicar," Percy Hacker, the verger, greeted him as he went into the vestry.

"Morning, Percy. Looks like we're in for another grand day."

"It does that," Percy replied. "And we're in for a good summer, too. As I came to church this morning, I spotted a wren building her nest in one of those branches overhanging the stream. Always the sign of a good summer, that is."

The vicar smiled to himself. He hadn't heard that one before. When it came to predicting the weather, Percy was a walking encyclopaedia. A mackerel sky, a halo round the moon, the oak out before the ash, cows lying down in a field, a cat

58

licking her fur, a squirrel with a bushy tail . . . All would tell him if the weather was set to be fair or foul.

Martin loved to hear Percy's accounts of country lore, but could never remember what the signs predicted. Did a mackerel sky mean he should take his umbrella or leave his raincoat on the hanger in the hall? Was the squirrel's bushy tail telling him to wear his battered old straw hat for protection from the sun or to wrap his scarf around him? So, whilst he would much rather have relied on Percy, reluctantly he had to make do with the weather forecast on the radio.

THE Reverend Martin Stratton had been vicar at St James's Church for well over twenty years and was fast approaching the time when he must think of retiring. He was greatly loved throughout the village, both by those who never went to church and those who made up his congregation. There were very few in the parish who hadn't been touched in some way by his kindness and concern over the years. Sharing their joys and their sorrows, he held a very special place in their hearts.

by Mikala Pope.

Illustration by Martin Baines.

59

All that said, it cannot be denied that when it came to sermons and making speeches, the Reverend Stratton was — not to put too fine a point on it — very long-winded and rather dull. But, knowing what to expect, the congregation always came prepared. Miss Atkins, from Grapevine Cottage, swore that an extra-extra-strong peppermint, surreptitiously popped into her mouth as the vicar climbed the pulpit steps, helped to keep her from nodding off. Although it was not to be commended, Bobby Brown, the youngest choirboy, had a comic hidden inside his hymn-book. And Mrs Joiner, doing her best to listen to the sermon, always had her left elbow at the ready to give her husband a dig in the ribs at his first snore.

Who, then, would have believed the reaction caused by the vicar's words on this particular Sunday? Miss Atkins almost swallowed her peppermint in surprise; Mr Joiner woke up with a start; and even young Bobby Brown looked up from his comic when he heard the gasp from around the church.

And then the whole congregation began to applaud, something never heard before in St James's.

AS Joyce pedalled her ancient bicycle down the lane that Sunday morning, the signs of early spring were everywhere: trees heavy with blossom, hedgerows bursting into leaf, and twittering birds busily gathering twigs to build their nests. She wheeled her bicycle through the ancient lychgate into the churchyard, a mass of golden daffodils, then took the little path that led to the back of the church.

She leaned her bicycle against the railings that led down to the room that housed the none-too-efficient coke boiler, then took the sheets of music from the wicker basket attached to the handlebars. Although almost ten years had gone by since she had taken over from Mr Granger, she still couldn't quite believe that she was the organist at St James's. After all, Mr Granger had been a proper organist, something she never considered herself to be.

Her thoughts drifted back to the day when the Reverend Stratton had called to ask whether she would be able to help out while they looked for a permanent organist. Her mother had recently died and Joyce was still not used to living on her own above their village shop.

She had just locked up for the day and was looking forward to a nice cup of tea when there was a knock on the door. The vicar, who had given her so much comfort and support over the last few weeks, explained the reason for his visit.

"But I couldn't play for services!" Joyce protested. "Mr Granger kindly let me practise on the organ, but I'm not good enough to play in public. I know I'd get into a right tizzy and play all the wrong notes."

"We'll all forgive the occasional tizzy and wrong note." The vicar chuckled. "And you really would be helping us out. Just until we find someone to take it on permanently," he added, using all his powers of persuasion.

And so, with much trepidation, Joyce had agreed and, ten years later, was still waiting for that permanent organist to arrive. Thankfully, there were now far fewer tizzies and wrong notes and, more importantly, she thoroughly enjoyed being the "temporary" choirmistress and organist.

Although running the village shop had been more than enough to keep her busy, on looking back, she could see that after she had been left alone, she had needed some other interest in her life apart from work. This had been the very thought in the vicar's mind when he'd approached her with his request.

"Morning, Miss Walters." Bobby Brown's cheerful greeting broke into her thoughts as she made her way back down the little path to the front of the church.

"In good voice this morning, Bobby?" she asked her youngest choirboy.

"'Course I am!" he replied, with that cheeky grin of his.

As Joyce followed Bobby into the church she at once felt that familiar sense of comfort. In a world that had changed so much, there was always something reassuring about this building which was much the same as when she had been christened here almost sixty years ago.

"Morning, Joyce," Percy greeted her.

"Hello, Percy." Joyce smiled. "They're working you hard this morning, aren't they? Since when has the verger given out the hymn-books?"

"Poor old Joe was on the rota to be a sidesman, but he's laid up with his lumbago again," Percy replied. "So I'm standing in for him this morning."

As Joyce settled herself at the organ, she was soon lost in thought again . . .

There couldn't be many people in the village of her and Percy's age who were still living in the same house where they were born. Percy was just a few months older than her and still lived in the cottage next door to the shop.

As children they had played together and always been in the same class at the village school. Even then, he'd been fascinated by all things to do with the countryside, and she smiled to herself as she recalled the time he'd got stuck in the oak tree on the village green, trying to see into a squirrel's drey. His dad hadn't been pleased to be called from work to rescue him.

Who would have thought, all these years later, she would end up as organist and Percy as verger?

Well, enough of daydreaming! The service would start soon and she hadn't finished sorting out her music yet.

PERCY smiled to himself as he handed Miss Charnock a hymn-book. Without fail, she was always last to arrive for the morning service, out of breath and huffing and puffing, even though she only lived two doors away from the church. It was just as well the vicar was always late starting or she would never make it in time.

As he waited for the service to begin, Percy's thoughts wandered back over the years, just as Joyce's had a few minutes ago.

After leaving school, he'd gone to work for Mr Langley at Longbarrow Farm, just outside the village. Ever since he'd been a little boy, he'd wanted to work on a farm and had soon displayed a natural gift for working with the farmyard animals, the pigs being his favourite.

As the years went by, you couldn't have found a man more content with his lot in life than Percy. Fully expecting to continue at Longbarrow Farm until he retired, in his late forties Percy's life had taken a dramatic change of direction. For, when his father died, he'd had to give up his work to look after his frail mother, becoming her full-time carer.

Devoted to his mother, Percy had never once questioned or regretted his decision to give up the job he loved, but the next few years had not been easy for him. As his mother needed someone to be with her at all times, he'd hardly ever left the cottage. On looking back, he wondered how he would have managed if it hadn't been for the kindness of Joyce, always ready to sit with his mother if he ever had to leave her for an hour or so.

Cooking, too, had been something of a problem. When his mother had first become poorly, his father had cooked all their meals, and Percy had never so much as boiled an egg. Although he'd done his best, there seemed to be more disasters in the kitchen than successes. Once again, Joyce had come to the rescue, assuring him whenever she brought round a casserole or apple pie that it required no more effort to cook for three than for one.

Still waiting for the service to begin, he chuckled to himself as he remembered that that hadn't been the first time he'd sampled Joyce's cooking. When she was a little girl her mother had taught her to cook. Fairy cakes and gingerbread men were her speciality then, and the little boy next door had been only too pleased to share them with her.

It was not long after his mother died that the vicar, rather concerned about Percy, had asked him if he would consider taking on the job of verger. Whilst always somewhat shy and never a great socialiser when working on the farm, Percy had enjoyed an occasional pint of beer in the village pub with his one or two good friends and had always looked forward to his weekly game of bowls. Although now in a position to do these things again, the past seven years had precluded any interests outside the home, and the vicar had sensed that he was finding it difficult to pick up the threads of his old life. He feared that there was a very real danger of Percy becoming something of a recluse and facing a lonely future.

"What do you think, then, Percy?" the vicar had asked, having broached the subject of him becoming verger.

"Oh, I don't know, Vicar," Percy replied, doubtfully shaking his head.

"There's more to it than the Sunday services, of course," the vicar continued. "There's the old coke boiler to contend with, for a start — that's almost a full-time job in itself. Then there's the churchyard. I'm afraid it's got into a bit of a state since Harry had to give up being verger. You really would be doing us a great favour if you could take it on, Percy."

And so Percy had agreed. Now, three years later, he could see that it was one of the best decisions he'd ever made. He really enjoyed the work, the churchyard had never looked better, and he'd got to know so many nice people. He did just sometimes wonder whether the vicar had asked him because . . .

The choir processing into the church put an end to his reminiscing.

"We begin our service this morning by singing hymn number three hundred and seventy-seven," the vicar announced. "'Let us, with a gladsome mind'."

Percy thought it couldn't have been a better choice.

∗   ∗   ∗   ∗

The service reached that point when Miss Atkins had just popped her extra-extra-strong peppermint into her mouth, Bobby Brown had found his comic, and Mrs Joiner's left elbow was getting ready for the snore. But, this morning, not peppermint nor comic nor elbow was needed.

There was a twinkle in the vicar's eye as he spoke the words that caused the gasp of surprise and then the applause. You might well have guessed what those words were, but they took everyone in the church by complete surprise — everyone, that is, apart from Joyce and Percy.

The words were these:

"I publish the Banns of Marriage between Joyce Walters, spinster of this parish, and Percy Hacker, bachelor of this parish. If any of you know cause, or just impediment, why . . ."

The vicar joined in the joyful applause that had interrupted him in mid-flow, then, smiling broadly, continued. ■

Always The Bridesmaid

ANOTHER glass of champagne, Lydia?" the elderly gentleman asked, getting up from his seat beside her.

"Oh, I shouldn't really."

"It is a celebration."

"Off you go, then." Lydia watched him go, taking the chance to reach up and check the cream and burgundy feathery accessory on her hair.

She was contented beyond belief. She couldn't believe the fortuitous happenings of the past few weeks, and all because of Hayley. Her eyes drifted to her great-niece swirling round the dance floor in the arms of Ross, her husband of five hours. Lydia had not expected this day to turn out to be so wonderful. For the bride and groom, yes, but not for herself, a maiden aunt.

"So how's it going, Aunt Lydia?" a young man asked. "Still stealing the limelight from the bride?"

"Oh, get away with you, James. Your eyes must be misty from watching your sister." Lydia accepted the compliment from her great-nephew with an inward preen of delight.

"Just don't forget you owe me a dance, Aunt."

"When I get my breath back," she said, patting her chest.

As he left her to mingle, Lydia's gaze returned to his sister.

Hayley was indeed a princess in her white satin dress with its structured bodice, crystal beading and laced-up back. A constant smile on those full red lips. Head tilted back, for her eyes had seldom left Ross since she'd met him at the altar.

If it hadn't been for Hayley's idea — so outlandish when she'd first mentioned it — this day would never have turned out so unbelievably well for Lydia. Hayley was such a special great-niece, just the sort of daughter she would have liked if things had turned out differently.

She found herself recalling the day, nine months before, when Hayley had approached her with that fanciful idea in mind.

✳   ✳   ✳   ✳

"What did you say?" Lydia had set the teapot back on the tray and had turned from the worktop to search Hayley's face for the seriousness of such an unheard-of proposal.

"I want you to be chief bridesmaid at my wedding next Easter. Ross is in total agreement, too."

"Wait now!" Lydia held her hands high to halt Hayley's enthusiasm. "Don't be ridiculous. I'm seventy!"

"Sit down. I've something to show you." Hayley drew from her shoulder bag a folded page from a newspaper. Smoothing it flat, she slid it before her great-aunt. "That's where I got the idea. That lady is your age."

Lydia stared at the photograph of the three bridesmaids clustered round the bride and groom on the steps of the church. It was the elated smile on the face of the elderly chief bridesmaid and how elegant she looked that held Lydia's gaze.

by Em Barnard.

Illustration by
Gerard Fay.

65

"As soon as I saw it, I knew it was the special way I'd been searching for to involve my favourite aunt," Hayley said, rising to pour the tea. As Lydia slowly shook her head, Hayley pushed on. "Where does it say there's an age limit on bridesmaids, tell me? After all, part of the bridesmaid's duties is to dress the bride on the day. And as you're making my dress, why, it makes sense."

Hayley set the mugs on the table to silence.

"What is it you're always quoting to all those brides you fit out at your shop? 'Always the bridesmaid, never the bride.' I know it's just a saying, Aunt, but you've never even been a bridesmaid. So it's about time you put that to rights."

SHE sat and caressed her aunt's wrist.

"I've always looked on you not just as my great-aunt, but as my fairy godmother, too. Since I was knee-high I've loved visiting your bridal wear shop. You used to allow me the off-cuts, remember? I spent hours dressing up in those silk and satin tatters.

"I want to repay you for all those wonderful moments, Aunt. So let me be your fairy godmother. Let me wave a wand over you and, well, if I could find you a handsome beau and transform you into a bride . . ." She trailed off, knowing her aunt's history. "But I can't. So share my wonderful day with me this way. Please, Aunt Lydia."

Lydia drew in a deep silent breath to steady her thudding heart at Hayley's mention of a beau. There had been a few along the way but no-one had captured her heart as Albert had. Not even Peter . . .

"We're not talking about long frilly dresses, Aunt. Something like in the photograph, a dress you can wear on other occasions. Like a christening," she added with a nudge, to lighten her aunt's downcast expression.

Lydia smiled.

"But I couldn't possibly sort out things like your hen party . . ."

"My two best friends, Carrie and Lynn, are taking care of everything else. Along with little niece Missy, they're going to be the other bridesmaids. There's no set rule for wedding duties these days.

"All I'm asking of you is to specialise in everything to do with the dresses — as you always promised you'd do when I married. After all, you have spent a lifetime designing, and fitting brides out for their special day."

Lydia had nodded to this fact.

"I'll take that as a promise, then. Brilliant, Aunt Lydia."

Before Lydia could argue the case, Hayley had begun chatting about other aspects of her wedding.

✳   ✳   ✳   ✳

"Aunt Lydia, I've dropped strawberries down my bridesmaid's dress," a small whining voice said.

Lydia came out of her reflecting and cast her eyes to the blue-eyed, angelic six-year-old before her.

"Oh, it's not that bad, Missy." She reached for a serviette and patted the red spot on the bodice.

"But it's spoiled now. I won't be able to wear it again."

"I've some special stuff in my shop that magics stains away," Lydia whispered, her eyes sparkling with secret knowing. "So you get your mum to bring you and the dress along next week, eh?"

It had the desired effect. The child's face filled with delight. Lydia had yet to meet a little girl that hadn't found her bridal shop an enchanting fairyland.

"Meanwhile, we'll pin one of these burgundy-red rosebuds over it," Lydia continued. She drew one from the table display. "There. Off you go."

The child popped a sticky kiss on Lydia's cheek and ran off. Lydia watched her go. She shook her head at the uncanniness of recent events. Even that small mishap had stirred a memory in her.

"There. Off you go, Lydia. No-one will notice." The schoolmistress had patted the white rose she'd quickly sewn on the bodice of Lydia's wedding dress.

"Good luck, Lydia."

"Thanks, Peter." Lydia smiled at the schoolboy hovering on a crutch, ankle bandaged, nearby. "There's always next year," she said.

She ran off, her small hand holding the rose in place. It covered the red streak the lipstick had made when slipping from her nervous hand. She came alongside another boy waiting in the wings.

"You look smashing, Lydia," Albert said. "Like a princess."

"You look like a prince, Albert."

"Right. We're on." Albert offered his arm, and Lydia rested a white gloved hand on it.

Heads high and in true royal fashion they dropped down the short curved stairway to the beats of the "Wedding March". They were eleven years old and acting the lead roles in a school play.

The stage in the assembly hall was set out in ballroom fashion, their classmates decked out as ladies and gentlemen of Victorian high society. This was the final scene where, after a swirling waltz, the final curtain bow would be taken.

Lydia and Albert had grown up together through the war years, living next door, and playing in the terraced streets with the local gang. This was the first time they'd seen each other scrubbed up and in such finery. It was a revelation to them both.

Whirling round to the waltz they'd patiently learned and now danced to perfection, their eyes held each other's as the play demanded. Their young hearts seemed to demand it, too, for they were oblivious to all surrounding them.

"One day, Lydia," Albert murmured, as they bowed at the curtain call, "I shall ask you to marry me."

Lydia gazed up at him, eyes wide in wonderment. Peter had never offered that.

The following day they were back on Station Street, scruffy and screaming, jeering and fighting. Often, in a quiet moment, Albert would whisper in her ear, "One day . . ." Then he'd saunter off, a secret smile of that promise on his face, while Lydia's held the blissful elation of first love.

When they were sixteen, the Station Street houses were condemned and their parents had to be rehoused. Coming home from the pictures one evening, Albert dropped a bombshell.

"Mum and Dad want to emigrate to Australia."

Lydia's eyes widened.

"But that's . . . that's the other side of the world, Albert!"

He gripped her hands.

"As soon as I'm old enough I'll come back. I promise."

They had their first kiss that night, under the viaduct — their last, the morning he left. As he walked away, her hand had reached out to him and she felt her young heart break.

A TOUCH on her hand and Lydia jumped from her musing.

"Hello, Hayley," she said as the bride took a seat beside her in a swish of satin. "You happy, sweetheart?"

"Ecstatic!" Hayley said, fanning her full skirt in royal fashion. "And you? Not that I need to ask." There was a twinkle in her eye, for Lydia's good fortune was family knowledge now.

"Ecstatic," Lydia echoed, and they both laughed.

"I must admit, I never envisaged my playing the fairy godmother would bring you so much happiness."

"We've both been very lucky, Hayley."

"And the dresses are just stunning. Thank you, Aunt Lydia."

"It was always to be my wedding present to you from the time I first held you as a baby."

"Though you didn't expect to be planning one for yourself, eh?"

Lydia gave her a bemused look.

"Oh, you mean this dress? No. In my wildest dreams I'd never have thought I'd have been your bridesmaid."

"Which just proves, Aunt, that you should never give up, even on the wildest of dreams. And the colour scheme works a treat, don't you think?" she said, changing tack. "Though I'm wondering if all four bridesmaids should have had burgundy dresses, rather than Missy in a cream one. She's

Children's Classics

"Little Women"
by Louisa May Alcott.

L ITTLE WOMEN" was first published in 1868 and became an overnight success. As well as being popular, it was also very well received critically, and was hailed as an instant classic.

The story of the four March sisters, Meg, Jo, Beth and Amy, struggling against poverty, adversity and their own character flaws, struck a chord with many. In the months following publication, Alcott was inundated with requests for a sequel . . . and so she obliged! Writing furiously for two and a half months, she produced "Good Wives" in 1869.

This was the second part of "Little Women", picking up the story three years on from part one. Both parts were published together as one volume in 1880.

It is generally agreed that the character of Jo, the second-eldest March sister (fifteen at the start of the story) is based on Louisa May Alcott herself. Jo is a tomboy, outspoken, and has to fight to control her hot temper throughout the story. And while the whole story mirrors much of Alcott's life, there are some differences — for example, unlike her fictional self, Jo, Alcott never married, and her father was a pacifist, unlike the March girls' father, who served as a chaplain in the Union Army.

The story of the March girls captured hearts and imaginations the world over with its timeless feel and themes of family relationships. Alcott produced two sequels which were equally successful and well-received: "Little Men" in 1871 and "Jo's Boys" in 1886.

All four books continue to be loved by girls and women everywhere more than one hundred and forty years after the first book's publication, and have been the inspiration for countless films, stage adaptations and TV series. ■

already stained it."

"Yes, I should have cottoned on to that when we were deciding. Unlike me not to take into account the messiness of little Missy."

"But, if I remember rightly, Aunt, you were rather preoccupied over your own dress," she said, smiling.

Three weeks before, Lydia had stepped into her shop — Wedding Belles. It was a double window affair just off the high street. She'd started there as a young trainee. When the owner retired many years later Lydia had bought the shop from her. But now, though she herself had, in the loose sense of the word, "retired", she had let it to a young woman.

Mia so reminded Lydia of herself at that age. Enthusiastic. Grades in art and design. Though not like in Lydia's day when the hands-on approach at that clothing factory — her previous job — were the only "grades" she'd acquired.

"Morning, Lydia," Mia said brightly, her plain black dress accentuated by an array of scarves and custom jewellery. "Hayley's arrived. I'll be through in a minute. I've almost finished with this young bride-to-be."

Lydia smiled a "good day" as she passed through into the back room.

"Hi, Aunt Lydia." Hayley took her in a hug. "Oh, I can't wait to try my dress on."

"So, do you like it?" Mia asked, arriving just as Hayley was admiring herself in her gown.

"It's absolutely gorgeous. You've excelled yourself, Aunt."

"I've had twenty-three years to work on it, Hayley."

"So, how are you getting on with the bridesmaids' outfits?" Hayley asked.

Mia, hovering round Hayley, noticed the smile fade from Lydia's face.

"Three of the bridesmaids' are completed, but . . ." She glanced at Lydia.

Hayley caught the exchange.

"Oh, Aunt, don't tell me you haven't started yours yet?" Hayley set pleading eyes on Mia.

"She won't let you down, Hayley," Mia said firmly. "I promise you."

R IGHT," Mia said. "Shop closed for the half day. Now let's make a start on your dress." She gave Lydia a no-nonsense look.

Lydia led the way to the small first-floor room that she kept for herself, the remaining rooms used as storage. Photographs and cuttings patterned the walls. In the centre was a long table with a sewing-machine amidst the trappings of a creative seamstress.

Mia spotted the remnants of burgundy material on the table.

"I hope this is a sign you've started your dress."

Lydia, having gone across to a wardrobe, now produced a dress on a hanger.

"You've made it!" Mia stared, open-mouthed.

Lydia clipped the hanger over the door and left Mia to review it while she sat on the sofa watching her.

Mia gazed over it with a professional eye. It was a neat A-line sleeveless dress in burgundy duchesse satin with a long-sleeved bolero jacket to match. The borders of neck and sleeves were edged with two narrow lines of cream piping, as were the false pockets.

"But why the secret, Lydia?"

"I didn't want to commit myself. Oh, I know that sounds silly, for I would never have let Hayley down. I suppose it was my sort of . . . safety valve."

Mia came and sat beside her.

"You're still doubtful about this, aren't you?"

Lydia nodded.

"I've spoken to all the family, especially the older ones. My sister, Lavinia, laughs in my face — she thinks I must be mad not to want to do it. None of them seem to understand, Mia. I . . ." She wrung her hands together. "I just don't want to look like mutton dressed as lamb."

"Oh, Lydia!" Mia grasped and stilled Lydia's restless hands. "Why, this is a family affair we're talking about. Everyone loves you." She sighed and bit her lip, gazing thoughtfully at Lydia. "The lady in the photograph who gave Hayley the idea. Why don't you go and see her?"

"I couldn't do that!"

"I found the bride through that photograph in the newspaper, Lydia. She's had a word with her grandmother and Mrs Hart would love to talk to you. I've got her address downstairs. It's twenty miles away, but I'll run you there. I'm sure it would set your mind at rest to talk to her."

Lydia sat in the dining-room of the bungalow of Dora Hart's house, with its cream walls, pale blue furnishings and mahogany furniture. They'd finished a cup of tea and now, beside her on the deep-blue suite, Dora held the wedding album open between them.

"It was to be my seventy-fifth birthday the week after the wedding, and as my granddaughter would be away on honeymoon she decided this was to be my special present from her and her new husband. Yes, I was apprehensive, too, but it was all unfounded," she said with a cheerful smile.

"It was more than just the day. It was all and everything to do with the wedding. I went to the dress fittings, helped choose the flowers, the favours. Ooh, it was wonderful being so much a part of it. And then the day itself. Helping her dress. Checking the gown at the church before she went down the aisle. At the top, I lifted her veil then held the bouquet. Oh, and walking back out on the arm of the best man, why, it was the icing on the cake.

"I didn't feel anywhere near my age, Lydia — in fact, I felt as young and beautiful as any bride in here." She patted her heart. "My Jim says he wanted to turn me round and take our vows again. No, Lydia, you grab it with both hands."

"But didn't you feel self-conscious?"

"Gracious, no. I had as many compliments as the bride." She turned another page in the album.

Lydia peered closer, her heart quickening.

"Who's that?"

"That's Albert, my brother-in-law."

"Albert Saunders?"

"You know Albert?"

"I did once. Before he went to Australia."

Dora stared at her guest.

"My goodness, Lydia! Of course. You must be the girl Albert left behind!"

Lydia returned Dora's surprise.

"He mentioned me?"

"Oh, yes. My family and his were billeted in the same camp when we first arrived in Australia. In fact, he rankled many of the kids going on about the girl he'd left behind. Why, we'd all left friends behind. But I remember mainly because from the first time we met, on the boat, June had a crush on him. That's my sister. The girl he eventually married."

Lydia sank back on the sofa, stunned.

Dora explained.

"I married a Brit. Jim and I didn't like Australia. We came home just before our first baby. Albert and June stayed." Dora refilled the cups, allowing the revelations to sink in. "My sister died a year ago. We persuaded Albert to come over for the wedding. He needed the break. His son lives in the States." She looked at Lydia. "Albert then decided he wanted to come home. For good."

LYDIA passed the cup of tea, taking another opportunity to look at the grey-haired man on her sofa. Slim and straight-backed, Albert was as much the self-assured man as he was once streetwise kid. When he smiled his thank you, it was like she'd gone back fifty years.

"It seems so strange to be sitting here with you, Lydia. Rather like all those years never came between us." He took a sip of tea.

Lydia sat in the chair opposite.

"I was upset when Peter told me you were courting someone else."

"You were all I cared about, Lydia. My letters should have told you that."

"You never mentioned her in your letters to me."

"There was no reason to."

"I presumed you were keeping her from me. And telling Peter was your easy way out."

Albert looked aghast.

York, England.

IF you asked my husband what he remembered about our family holidays to York, I know exactly what he would say. He would tell you, in great detail, about the National Railway Museum. He would also tell you that it was the children who loved it really and that he only went along to keep them company!

My memories of York are slightly different and I have to say that the time they all spent at the National Railway Museum meant that I could get away by myself and explore this lovely city on my own. York for me is lovely scenery, cafés and shops that I could wander through at my own pace, taking my time and enjoying myself.

It didn't stop me meeting the rest of the family back at the museum, though, and having a go on the mini train. That definitely was fun!

— *Mrs Y.L., Peterhead.*

J. CAMPBELL KERR.

"Is that what you believed?"

"I didn't know what to believe. Put it down to an inexperienced heart. You were on the other side of the world with her and, well, Peter had always been waiting in the wings, we both knew that. So when he took the advantage and proposed, I accepted. Next you wrote back congratulating us and saying you'd also found someone."

"I hadn't, at the time. I just didn't want you believing you'd left me broken-hearted." He dipped his head.

"And June?"

"She'd been like a thorn in the side." He smiled fondly. "She'd been after me since we stepped aboard the boat."

"But you loved her."

"Yes. And you? You didn't marry Peter?"

"No. It wouldn't have been fair on him. I didn't truly love him."

"So what happened? We lost touch after that."

"I left the factory. I moved here, shared the flat above with a girlfriend. Trainee in a bridal wear shop. The irony of it, eh?" Lydia smiled. "But believe it or not, I loved every minute. Working with silks and satins rather than denim, it lifted the heart no end. Has done ever since."

"No-one else came along?"

"No-one that rose above my work."

"Lydia . . ." Albert had hesitated. "Is there a chance that we could meet up now and then? It would give me great pleasure to take you places, see you smile, hear your laughter again."

Lydia had nodded.

"That would be nice, Albert."

＊　　＊　　＊　　＊

"Your champagne, Lydia."

"Thank you, Albert."

"It's rather hot in here. Shall we take a stroll round the grounds when you've drunk up?"

Stepping into the glorious sunshine of an April day, they strolled along the pea-shingled pathways that angled between the velvet lawns of the stately hotel.

"Remember that school play when we were kids? Do you remember the curtain call, what I said to you?" He stopped and took her hands in his. "I don't want that promise to fall by the wayside as the other did. It's still early days, but from the moment you opened your door my heart grew young again. So, if I was to say to you, Lydia . . . One day . . ."

Lydia saw again that secret promise in his eyes, while Albert saw in hers the blissful elation of true love. They strolled on, sure in the knowledge that shortly, one day, that promise would be fulfilled. ∎

by Jean Syme.

Illustration by
David Young.

Hokey-cokey Weather

GINTY was still tired when she woke up. She slapped the curtain back and looked out of the window at the crab-apple tree. Its branches, still hung with bright red fruit, scratched at the glass. The leaves were dying embers, lifting themselves from the branches, then huddling and squirming on the ground like landed fish.

Ginty turned to look in the dressing-table mirror. The angle was wrong for vanity. Clear, honest daylight lit the furrows and lines around her eyes and brows. Her hair, an uncompromising grey, framed her face. She peered closely at herself, then stood up straight and rummaged in the drawer for her favourite soft woolly jumper.

75

Once she'd pulled it over her head, she looked again towards the window, smiled, and gave her head a jerk. Ginty looked like a woman who had made a decision.

It seemed a long time since that day in spring when the Clarks had moved in next door. Andy had been coming down the path, smiling as usual.

"It's that hokey-cokey weather again — sun in, sun out," he greeted her. "Rain on, rain off. Wind up, wind down — doing the hokey-cokey." He winked at Ginty as he handed over her letters.

"I see you're getting new neighbours again," he continued. "Nothing but change." He walked quickly back towards his van, lifting his hand in farewell.

Andy had been a small boy when he'd come to Scotland with his parents, uncle and aunt and two sisters. His name was Andeep but the village welcomed him and his smile, called him Andy, and took change from his tiny, serious fingers in the newspaper shop his parents had bought.

"He's fairly coming on," the villagers would say. "He's taken to the language like a duck to water."

Andy would nod, delighting the old men as they collected their papers.

"Like a duck to water," he'd repeat.

GINTY glanced through her mail and then peered over the fence. At long last, after two years, it appeared she was to have permanent neighbours. The furniture van was already parked at the house next door. It had been closely followed by a blue car with what looked to be two children in the back seat.

Ginty adjusted her specs and tried to see more clearly but the car was partially obscured by the beech hedge which had grown too tall for her to see over.

The hedge had become a bit of a nuisance, for the east wind blew the autumn leaves on to Ginty's driveway. Reluctant leaves had waited well into winter to fall and still lay now, in early spring, damp and dark, sad reminders of brighter days.

It would be good to have her old friend Bessie's home filled with the clamour of children.

Since Bessie died, Ginty had had disappointing neighbours. Bessie's great-nephew, to whom she had left her house, had been undecided about what to do with it and it had been rented out furnished. The tenants seemed careless and indifferent, birds of passage who needed no human bond in the village and had no commitment to looking after the house or garden.

Ginty had initially ventured a greeting or an offer of help to the new tenants, but had given up. For all of them it had been a passing place, a stopover on the way to something better or more permanent. In the meantime Bessie's home seemed to become smaller, shabbier, unloved, the windows dull and the dustbins permanently overflowing.

Andy, who had, as he said, his ear well cocked, kept Ginty informed about her neighbours' movements.

"Leaving next week," he informed her, as more ramshackle boxes stifled the driveway. "And let's hope they take everything with them, including that rusty old car in the garden."

The previous week a band of cleaners had come in and Bessie's great-nephew, Ben, had come up from England and visited Ginty.

He thanked her for her kindness to his great-aunt and said he had reluctantly decided to sell. He had thought he might rent out the house until he retired and then come back to Scotland to live, but the rentals were proving too much of a problem.

"I'll try to make sure it's someone that you can chat to." Ben smiled at her. "I know how much you and Aunt Bessie used to enjoy a blether."

"It's not just for the chat I miss her," Ginty said. "She always had such an interesting life. Even the year she died, she was away adjudicating at a music festival in Leeds. She always had a tale to tell about her work and her visits to friends in so many different places."

Ben's face had the same expression of kind concern that Bessie's had had.

"I've put all the furniture into storage in the meantime," he said. "I want to have a good look at it first. I'm afraid there's been some damage done by the people that rented.

"One thing, though," he continued. "Aunt Bessie wanted you to have a picture. You know — the one that hung above the piano."

It was of Florence, quite a small picture, no more than eighteen inches square, but filled with golden light. It was of a house, an ordinary town house, two storeys high with a balcony on the top floor. You could tell the balcony was often used, even though it was empty of people. Glasses stood on a small table, a cloth hung over the railings, untidy plants sent feelers through the rails. Soon someone would wake from their afternoon sleep and, holding a cup of coffee and a book ready to fall open, bring the balcony back to life.

The window on the ground floor was shuttered against the heat of the sun.

"I lived there once," Bessie had told Ginty. "For a while it was my home. I was studying in Florence and I shared it with another student."

On the rare evenings when Bessie and Ginty ate together, Bessie would play and the picture of Florence above the piano seemed to absorb the music, making it a house of sun and sound, busy with happy conversations.

Ginty hung it on her bedroom wall and often looked at it before going to sleep, imagining Bessie there.

✳   ✳   ✳   ✳

Summer came and Ginty became familiar with the neighbours, Judith and Colin, and their two boys. She knew their routines of school and home, their weekend busyness in the garden, the mêlée of footballs and boys and voices that wove patterns of anger, pleasure, dismay, triumph.

Ginty had been made welcome in their home but the change was disorientating. There was no such thing as a quiet cup of tea there!

Sometimes it seemed as though the house would burst. A quantity of trainers, lying as they had been kicked off, were scattered at the front door. In the kitchen, the table held a spill of packages of food or an array of jotters, books and pencils.

"Come through to the sitting-room," Judith would say. "We can't seem to find a clear space in here."

The sitting-room was always tidy, but sparse. Black leather couches, a wooden floor, a neat rug, a silent television in the corner.

Judith breathed a sigh.

"This is our peaceful room." She smiled at Ginty. "You must have gone through this as well."

Ginty nodded.

"A boy and a girl."

But Bessie, who had never had children, wouldn't recognise this room now. Bessie's room had been soft and cosy and vibrant, all blues and purples. There had always been vases of flowers when she was at home; always books and letters on the desk, music open on the piano stand.

*   *   *   *

Andy handed Ginty a handful of letters and postcards.

"Where are you going for your holiday knees-up this year?" He did a couple of dance steps at the doorway.

"Spain. With my son and family as usual. I'll be away from the fifth for two weeks."

"I'll keep an eye open for you. Or —" he turned back to look at Ginty "— I could come and stay in your house for a bit of peace and quiet. How about it? I could snatch forty winks."

Ginty laughed. The whole village knew Andy's extended family, their good-natured noise and cheerfulness.

Time To Play

A BUSY day — so much to do —
I didn't care the sky was blue
And golden sunshine seemed to say,
"Don't skulk indoors — it's time to play!"
But household chores held far more weight,
Till something made me hesitate,
As through the window, way up high,
I glimpsed a creamy butterfly;
And then another — yes, a pair —
Were dancing, dancing in the air!
I set my dusters to one side,
I left my broom and ran outside,
Those tiny insects changed my ways;
Life's much too short to waste such days!

— *Maggie Ingall.*

The fortnight in Spain went quickly. Ginty saw little of her grandchildren during the day. They swam in the pool that was shared by the visitors in the chalets, or they were off doing some organised activity. Her son, Stephen, and his wife, Fiona, seemed only to want to relax, which was understandable, since they both had busy full-time jobs. Ginty, therefore, spent a lot of time wandering around the town itself.

She enjoyed meandering around the narrow streets, listening to the strange voices, smelling the sea, the fish, the coffee, feeling the sun reach right inside her. She enjoyed cold, fresh orange juice in cool, dark cafés, and reading in the shelter of a large rock on the beach.

In the late afternoon she would go back to the chalet, prepare a meal for the family and play games afterwards with the children when their parents went out for a drink or a walk in the sultry evening.

"You don't mind?" Stephen asked.

"Mind what?"

"Being on your own so much?"

"I enjoy it. Really, I do. But you don't need me with you on holiday now, do you? The children are getting older and more and more independent."

Fiona looked upset.

"We don't just want you for your help. We like your company."

"I know that," Ginty reassured her. "I just feel I'm ready to branch out more on my own. I've just realised that there are lots of things I've never done."

Stephen and Fiona exchanged anxious glances. They had often talked about Ginty, about her being on her own.

"After all," Stephen had said, "she's spent most of her life having someone to look after. Latterly she was doing a lot of looking after Bessie." He'd paused. "We must make sure she feels needed."

ANDY ran after her as she came out of the grocer's.

"Mrs Ross, Mrs Ross, I got your postcard. It looks a fine place. Did you enjoy yourself? Was it always sunny there?"

"It was lovely, Andy."

"But you look sad, Mrs Ross."

"Not really sad. It's just — I think I'll not go with the family next year."

"A new chapter. An empty page. That's wonderful. Every day you will do what you want to do." Andy's face lit with pleasure at the thought of such freedom.

*   *   *   *

Summer mellowed into autumn. Ginty was restless. She met friends regularly in the village tearoom, drove to the library in Perth every week for her clutch of detective stories, got a lift every Friday night to choir practice with another friend, but the early dark, the comfort shawl of coal fire and safely closed door, no longer brought contentment.

One week late in October, the library advertised a course for beginners in Italian. Clutching the leaflets, she collared Andy one morning on the doorstep.

"Easy to learn a new language?" Andy laughed. "Easy-peasy! How long does it take a baby to learn? Two years, maybe? And you understand them. Five years and you want them *not* to understand!"

"You think I should have a go, then?"

"My father didn't speak a word of English, not a word, when he came here. Now listen to him! And look at me! I am especially fluent," he added, with charming immodesty.

It was just after that that Ginty made her decision. She phoned Stephen and Fiona to let them know of her plans. After all, it was only polite.

She was clearing up the fallen leaves on her path when her son arrived. He was alone and that was ominous.

"Mum, what do you mean, you're going on your own?" he asked over a cup of coffee. "You've never been on holiday on your own."

"That's the point: I've never been on my own. You've never let me since your father died. But I'm perfectly capable of going on my own. And, as you said, this summer I was on my own most of the time."

Stephen was not to be placated.

"We all know you've really been missing Bessie, but —"

"— but don't start acting like a befuddled old woman?" Ginty completed his sentence.

"No, I don't mean that." Stephen forced himself to speak calmly.

"Mum, you're sixty-five. You've never been on your own in a strange place, is what I mean, a place where you don't know anyone.

"We've heard you speak a lot about Florence and Bessie and how much you'd like to go. Why don't you wait until spring? We'll look for a place near Florence which the kids would enjoy and we could all go together."

"Stephen, I'm not going to a place where I know no-one."

"I thought you were going to Florence?"

"You've misunderstood. I want to go to Florence when my Italian is passable, but I'm not ready for that yet."

"Sorry. I thought when you phoned to say you had decided to take a winter break on your own, that you had decided to go to Florence." Stephen looked relieved.

"Oh, that. That was just the beginning. That was what gave me the notion. I must admit I did think a lot about Bessie, about her travels on her own, about me stuck here like an old woman with nothing better to do. I looked a lot at her picture. Sometimes I imagined she was sending me a message."

Stephen looked uncomfortable.

"We don't think of you as an old woman," he muttered.

Ginty looked straight at him.

"Neither do I." She stood up and collected some leaflets from her desk.

LOOK at these and see what you think. I've booked up to go to India." Stephen sat silent, looking at Ginty's calm face.

"I'm flying from Manchester to Delhi to stay in a posh hotel for a weekend. Andy recommends it."

"Delhi? For a weekend?"

"And then on up into the hills where it'll be cooler. I'll be staying in a smaller hotel, but there'll be plenty of people to look after me."

"Who?"

"All of Andy's family."

"Andy?"

"Yes, Andy the postman. There's no use looking like that, Stephen. It's all arranged. There's no point in looking backwards. It's up, up and away — tallyho, as Andy's father says."

"Mum! What if something happens to you?"

"You mean, if I take ill, or get mugged? It could happen anywhere. It could have happened when I was walking around Spain."

"But we worry about you."

"As you used to say to me when you were a boy, 'Don't worry, I'll be all right.' And you were.

"Andy has looked after me ever since Bessie died. He makes sure he hears me or sees me every time he delivers a letter or passes my door. It's his nature. He knows everyone in the village who's on their own. I trust him."

There was a long silence while they looked despairingly at one another. Ginty spoke.

"Andy's father says, 'If you face the sun, don't look back for you'll see only shadows'." Ginty leaned over to touch Stephen's arm.

"I know you care. But don't worry." She walked towards the window and looked out at the wind huffing and puffing at the berries.

"Besides, Stephen, I'm very lucky. I'll be able to escape this awful hokey-cokey weather." ■

Everything's Coming Up Roses

I'D come to Long Morton to find some peace and quiet and work on the book. No, let's be honest — I'd come to get away from Carl. I hadn't said anything to him beforehand. I'd just looked around, found this perfectly lovely cottage and made a quiet getaway. It hadn't been difficult. Carl was otherwise occupied with the delectable Melanie from Marketing and had far too much on his mind to be concerned about the sudden disappearance of an ex-girlfriend.

The trouble was I still loved him. Everything in Rowhampton reminded me of him. We'd shared the same friends, we'd worked at the same publishers, we'd belonged to the same clubs and we'd done everything together. Everyone had expected we would get married — including me. However, it turned out that Carl had other plans, so I'd decided to make a clean break, put a healthy number of miles between us and settle down to make a fresh start.

I'd been so lucky to find Larch Cottage. Because of its somewhat dilapidated condition, it was being offered at a rent I could just about afford. It had everything; roses round the door, low-beamed ceilings, a huge open fireplace in the living-room and a range in the kitchen. The fact that the roses were an overgrown tangle, the fireplace was draughty and the range smoked and had to be stoked regularly to prevent it going out detracted from its charms not one jot. I loved it the minute I saw it.

I advertised in the local paper, asked around in the village and phoned a few old contacts, and managed to find enough freelance illustration work to keep the wolf from the door until the book I was illustrating was finished.

I set up my desk under the window where the light was good and where I could look out on the jungle that I suspected had once been a pretty cottage garden. Who had created it, I wondered. I imagined someone digging the ground and choosing plants; someone who cared for it and loved it. I found myself doodling on scraps of paper as I worked, sketching its framework of cobbled paths and the trellis arch that sagged across the front gate, then filling in the beds with colourful flowers. Was this what it once looked like?

Channel hopping on TV one evening, I found "Gardeners' World". They just happened to be starting a new project; rescuing an overgrown and neglected garden. The next day I called at the library and gathered an armful of gardening books. I was going to restore my tangled plot to its former glory.

Carl would have thought I was mad. There was nothing he hated more than getting his hands dirty. He was an artist, he would say. His hands were his livelihood. A little gremlin inside me suggested that maybe it had just been an excuse to avoid anything resembling hard work.

From then on, I spent every spare moment in the garden. I dug, pruned and composted everything I could lay my hands on, and what I lacked in technique, I made up for with enthusiasm. I had a new mission in life and I was determined to succeed.

I suppose every village has its leading light, its person who "gets things done". Long Morton has Julie. Julie can be very persuasive when she sets her mind to something, and this particular day her mind was firmly set on getting Long Morton into the famous "The Yellow Book", which lists thousands of

by Gail Crane.

*Illustration by
Mark Viney.*

gardens, most of them privately owned, which open to visitors on a certain days to raise money for charity.

"Come on, Dinah," she cajoled, talking to me over the gate as I weeded a flower-bed. "You'll love it. Madge, Joanne and Maria have already agreed and five would be so much better than four."

I couldn't quite see the logic behind that, but I let it pass. It's useless to argue with Julie when she's in full swing.

"I'm just not sure that I want to have people wandering round, that's all," I replied. "And I really don't have the time at the moment. I have drawings to finish and deadlines to meet."

"But there's plenty of time. It won't be for months yet and your garden looks absolutely great already. I mean, it's just amazing how much you've achieved since you've been here."

Not only is Julie persuasive, she is also an inveterate flatterer when she thinks it will serve her purpose. She was right. I *was* enjoying it immensely, but my garden was my own private place and I wanted to keep it that way.

"I'll think about it," I conceded, in the vain hope that if I prevaricated long enough, I might somehow be let off the hook. No chance!

"Wonderful! We're having a meeting on Thursday evening to discuss everything — my place at seven o'clock. See you there!"

Much to my surprise, by Thursday morning I found I was actually looking forward to the meeting. Having had a couple of days in which to mull things over, I was feeling quite motivated by the idea. Yes, it would be hard work, but it would also be a challenge and my life could certainly stand some excitement.

I WALKED home after the meeting feeling really enthusiastic. Julie worked her charm on the rest of the village and by the time the day of the first inspection arrived she had recruited a further four people. She was ecstatic when we all passed.

"Well, ladies, we've done it," she told us excitedly. "Now it's all hands to the trowels and the lawnmowers. Nothing less than perfection will do for the village of Long Morton."

Thus began weeks of frenetic activity. Plants were exchanged, tools loaned, advice and help freely given, and a feeling of communal effort and purpose developed throughout the village. People who had never spoken more than a passing word or two to each other stopped to talk and pass on the latest progress reports and I was as caught up in the excitement as everyone else.

"I said you'd enjoy it, didn't I," Julie reminded me one day as she passed a tray of seedlings across the fence. "Oh, and Madge asked if you could let her have some of your geranium cuttings if you have any left."

As she hurried off, I wondered where she found her energy. When I wasn't working at the drawing-board, I was waging war on rampant weeds and chomping insects, and most nights I fell into bed, exhausted.

I decided to take the geraniums round to Madge before lunch.

There was no answer to my knock so, assuming she was out, I went through the side gate, intending to leave the plants in the back garden.

ELLO, there," a deep voice said from behind a buddleia bush. "Oh, I'm sorry," I apologised, jumping in surprise. "I didn't realise anyone was here. I just wanted to leave these for Madge."

He came across the lawn towards me, smiling.

"That's OK. Come on in. My sister has taken herself off to town for the morning, but she shouldn't be long.

"I'm Eddie," he continued, holding out a rather grubby hand. "Sorry about the dirt."

"I'm Dinah, and don't worry, mine are just as bad," I replied, thinking what a nice firm handshake he had. He had nice blue eyes, too . . .

"I assume you are involved in this scheme of Julie's that seems to have taken hold of half the village?"

"I'm afraid so. She's got us all running round like mad things."

"How true that is. Look at me! I only came down for a quiet weekend to relax and catch up with the newspapers, and what happens? I get roped in to weed the garden." He grinned. "Actually, I'm quite enjoying it."

"So am I, though I haven't confessed to it yet." We exchanged conspiratorial smiles.

I nodded towards the tray of plants I was still holding.

"Where shall I put these?"

"Ah, yes." He pointed to the terrace. "I think over there would be fine. Tell me," he continued as I deposited the plants, "which garden is yours?"

"Larch Cottage."

"You mean that dilapidated place at the end of Back Street?"

"Even you might look a bit worse for wear if you had been neglected for years," I retorted. Then I had to laugh. "You're absolutely right. It is in rather a state, isn't it?"

"It's sad, really. When Madge and I were children it was owned by an old chap called Fred. I suppose he must have been retired because he seemed to spend all day in that garden. Winter or summer, rain or shine, he'd be out there digging and planting. Since he died it's been let to various people, but none of them stayed long, which is why it's become so neglected."

"Well, it's a whole lot better now than when I moved in." Without stopping to think, I added, "You should come and have a look."

I hadn't *actually* meant to say that. Larch Cottage was my private retreat and the last thing I wanted at the moment was to get involved with another man, even if he did have nice eyes.

Eddie's face lit up.

"I'd love to," he said. "I'm not actually doing anything right now if —"

I cut in before he could go any further.

"You've got all this weeding to do . . . and I'm afraid I have to get back to work. You know, deadlines and things."

"Ah, yes. Madge said you were an artist."

"Illustrator. I illustrate children's books." I turned to go. "Anyway, some other time, maybe?"

"Yes, sure. I'll look forward to it." He held out his hand. "It's been nice meeting you."

The feel of his hand sent a little shiver of attraction through me. It had been nice meeting him, too, and I felt a twinge of regret that I hadn't been more encouraging.

For the next few days every bit of free time was taken up with planting, weeding and staking and all the while my thoughts drifted back to a deep-voiced man with a charming smile and lovely blue eyes. I found myself wondering if he was thinking about me or whether he had forgotten all about me. If he had, I told myself, I could only blame myself.

That might have been the end of it if it hadn't been for the gale that blew in one night. I went into the garden the following morning, after a sleepless night listening to the wind buffeting the cottage, to find two branches hanging precariously from one of the big old apple trees. Clearly something would have to be done before we opened to the public, but what?

I might have known that Julie would have the answer.

"No problem," she said when I mentioned it to her, and the next day I looked out to see two men in helmets and safety goggles, equipped with a chainsaw, inspecting the tree. One was Julie's husband, Pat, and the other was Eddie.

Just looking at him made my heart beat faster. This was ridiculous — I had only met him once!

I HAD to complete and deliver a piece of work by midday and I couldn't afford to let this particular client down, so after thanking them both and making them coffee, I left them to it, promising to be back in time for lunch.

Julie arrived just as I got home, bringing sandwiches for us all. I found a bottle of wine and we sat in the garden, eating and chatting and soaking up the sunshine. I learned that Eddie was a botanist; quite an important one, it seemed, as he was head of his department at the local university.

I couldn't help being conscious of his nearness. It was almost as though an electric charge was zinging between us and I was sure that he was aware of it, too. Every now and then our eyes met and he smiled and my heart jumped. I had never felt that way with Carl.

The sandwiches were finished and the last drop of wine drained and Julie declared that she had to go and get on. I walked with them to the gate. Julie and Pat said goodbye and made their way back to their own house but Eddie

PS Waverley *On The Clyde, Glasgow, Scotland.*

*M*Y father worked as a young apprentice on the new
PS Waverley at the A. & J. Inglis shipyard in Glasgow. He
was very proud to have worked on the 693-tonne paddle steamer
and never stopped talking about it. My friends used to look alarmed
and start making excuses about having to go when he started
reminiscing, but my brothers and I were fascinated and loved to
hear all his stories about it.

My brothers in particular used to love hearing about its
predecessor, also called the PS Waverley, which took part in the
WWII war effort as a minesweeper and was sunk in 1940 while
helping with the evacuation of troops from Dunkirk.

It wasn't until we were adults that we fully appreciated my father's
part in history and I must admit to feeling a certain amount of
pride when I saw your cover. Thank you for the wonderful memory!
— *Mrs J.O'R., Largs.*

J. CAMPBELL KERR.

lingered, apparently reluctant to make the move.

"Thank you so much for your help," I said eventually. "I could never have managed that on my own."

"Well, you know where I am if you need any more help with the heavy stuff." His voice was husky. Then, quite unexpectedly, he dropped a kiss on my cheek and was gone.

I found it impossible to concentrate on work after that. I sat at my desk, gazing out of the window, my thoughts in turmoil. Eddie was so different from Carl and I found myself comparing the two of them. In almost every way Carl came out second-best. If I was honest, I had to admit that there was still a part of me that missed him. He was attractive and fun to be with and we'd had some good times together. Ever since leaving Rowhampton I'd believed I still loved him, but since meeting Eddie I was no longer so sure.

FOR a couple of days I was head down at the drawing-board and saw no-one, then I opened the door one morning and there was Eddie, smiling at me from behind a huge tray of cuttings.

"I've been roped in to deliver plants to everyone and these are for you," he said. "Where would you like me to put them?"

"Oh, just down there by the step will be fine. I'll move them later. Thanks." He'd really caught me off guard and I couldn't think of anything else to say.

He put them down and stood up, rubbing his back.

"You're my last delivery so I'm now off duty, so to speak, and I wondered if you'd like to come and have coffee with me. They do a passable cup at the Bell."

And so I found myself sitting in front of a log fire telling Eddie all about Carl and Melanie. I wasn't sure that I'd made much sense but he seemed to understand and it was such a relief to talk about it. I realised that, until now, I hadn't actually told anyone else how I felt. He put down his coffee cup and rested his hand on mine, apparently unaware of the effect it had on me.

"We can just be friends, you know," he said gently. "It doesn't have to get serious. Why don't we just take it easy and see where it goes?"

"I'd like that," I told him.

"How about dinner tonight to cement the friendship? No strings. No commitments."

It sounded wonderful. If only I didn't have to deliver some work to a client.

"I'd love to," I assured him. "The only thing is I need to make an early start tomorrow. I have to take some artwork to Rowhampton and it's going to take me most of this evening to finish it."

"Then we'll make a date for when you get back. There are only a couple of weeks until the big garden day, so I'll be here that weekend. Why don't we celebrate then?"

And so it was arranged. Like Eddie said, there was no need to get serious;

we could just enjoy each other's company as friends. I went to bed that night feeling happier than I had for some time. The only cloud on the horizon was the trip to Rowhampton. What feelings would that stir up, I wondered.

It felt really strange to be getting off the train at Rowhampton station. I'd forgotten how noisy and busy it was; so different from the peace and quiet of Long Morton. I took the bus to the centre of town and arrived at my client's office with time to spare. I was sitting in the reception area, head down reading a magazine to pass the time when I heard, "Hi, Di."

I felt the blood rush to my face and my heart began to pound uncontrollably. Only one person had ever greeted me like that.

Willing my voice not to shake, I looked up and said, as calmly as possible, "Hello, Carl."

He looked pleased to see me.

"Di, what brings you here? I thought you had left us for good." He slid into a seat next to me and I felt the old familiar flutter in my chest. Heavens, I'd really thought I had got over him but here he was, having the same old effect on me.

"I'm surprised you noticed," I said quietly. "Last time I saw you, you seemed to have other things on your mind."

"Ah." He did have the grace to look a little sheepish. "You mean Melanie, I suppose? Yes, well, we all make mistakes, and I'm afraid Melanie was one of mine. We went our separate ways some time ago."

I was shocked at the almost callous way he spoke of her.

"Is that what you told people about me as well?" I asked sharply.

"I'd never say that about you, Di. You and I were meant for each other, I can see that now. We should never have parted."

I was too stunned to speak. How could he sit there and say such rubbish?

"How about having lunch together when you finish here?" he continued. "Or maybe we could make it dinner one day. Where are you living now?"

I COULDN'T believe that after leaving me as he had, he thought he could just turn on the charm and I would be ready to pick up where we'd left off. My eyes were now well and truly open. If he could be so heartless about Melanie, he would be just the same with any other girl he became involved with. Again I found myself comparing him with kind, thoughtful Eddie — and there was no comparison at all.

"I don't think so," I told him, my voice cold as ice.

"Don't play hard to get, Di. Come on, you know what good times we used to have."

Luckily for Carl, the receptionist called my name just then. Don't play hard to get, indeed! Instead, I calmly picked up my portfolio, looked him straight in the eye and quietly said, "Goodbye, Carl," and walked away.

When I came out he had gone. I caught the train home with a feeling of release. I was ready to move on. Eddie, I thought, here I come.

The day finally dawned. I felt the first shiver of nervous excitement as I crawled out of bed at six o'clock, threw on my old gardening clothes and went down to eat an early breakfast. Not only was it "open garden" day, but I had dinner with Eddie to look forward to that evening.

I shuffled into my old gardening shoes, grabbed a sandwich and a mug of coffee, and went out to inspect the garden for any weeds that might have sprouted over night. Satisfied that everything was as perfect as I could make it, I fixed the *Garden Open* sign to the side gate.

The school car park was soon full, and by halfway through the afternoon, our narrow village streets were groaning with the overflow. I doubted whether Long Morton had ever before seen so many people at one time.

The afternoon flew by and I was feeling as trampled as the grass by the time the church clock chimed six and the last group of people was leaving. What a relief to be able to kick off my shoes and collapse into a garden seat.

Sacred Garden

I **KNOW** a sacred garden
Where one can find release
From care and wildest worries,
A place of rest and peace.

It's full of summer sunshine
And leaping hopes of spring.
Its autumn's filled with colour
And perfumes filtering.

The birds sing in my garden
In simple harmony
That points to choral music
Of birdsong symphony.

I LAY back and closed my eyes. The evening sun was still warm on my face and the hum of bees in the lavender and the chattering of sparrows round the bird table was hypnotic. I became increasingly drowsy until my eyes began to close and, in that half-dreaming state between wakefulness and sleep, I heard the gate open.

"Hello, friend."

I looked up and there was Eddie, smiling down at me.

"Hello, friend," I replied contentedly. "Come and sit down." I moved along the seat to make room for him beside me and immediately felt the same old charge zinging between us. He was feeling it, too. I could tell from the way he looked at me.

"So how did it go?" he asked.

90

Deep rust and yellowing foliage
Will wilt in winter's reign,
And clouds exude their showers,
But spring will shine again.

— *Margaret Comer.*

"It was wonderful. I really enjoyed it. But I'm glad it's over," I added with a wry grin. "My feet are killing me."

"You should see Julie. She's like the proverbial cat that got the cream. You'd think she had done the whole thing by herself."

I laughed.

"Well, it was her idea and it was her enthusiasm that got us all going, so I suppose she has a right to feel pleased with herself."

"I think everyone has done brilliantly, especially you. What you have done to this garden is nothing short of a miracle."

I glowed with pride at his praise.

"You're biased," I told him.

"Of course I'm biased." His voice had become husky with emotion and we looked at each other without speaking for what seemed like for ever. "I know we promised to be just friends, but do you have any idea how I feel about you?"

He had reached out and placed his hand on my arm and I suddenly knew that he was going to kiss me. And I knew, without a doubt, that I wanted him to.

When we came up for air a few minutes later, he put his hand under my chin and gave me a quizzical look.

"Whatever has happened since I last saw you? Or perhaps I shouldn't ask?"

I told him, very briefly, about my meeting with Carl.

"Let's just say I've had my eyes opened in more ways than one."

"Well, I'm very glad."

I looked into his beautiful blue eyes and his kind, smiling face and knew that he could hope for a great deal more than friendship. What I felt for Eddie was unlike anything I had ever felt before, and now I wasn't afraid to admit it. He must have read the answer in my expression.

I turned my face to his and just before our lips met again he whispered, "I love you."

As he took me in his arms I murmured, "I love you, too." And this time I had no doubts at all. ■

We'll Meet Again

by Sally Wragg.

DOES Jake Connors love me? The jolting train prompts my thought flow. I lean back against the seat, still trying to work it out. He loves me. He loves me not. I rather think he doesn't. He said he did once, so long ago now that I wonder if I dreamed it.

Smoke curls against the window. We gather speed, plunging into darkness, my reflection in the glass turning to Jake's, his eyes full of humour and that other thing always there every time he looks my way. He grins. I grin back, thankful the carriage is empty and no-one sees my foolishness. Another, smaller image joins him, a child, a replica of me with wild curls and freckles. An unruly child, unbidden and unbiddable.

My hand tightens, leaps to my mouth. How my mind spins back and how I long to be how I was then, at the start of the war. At the start of me and Jake. At the start of everything . . .

✳   ✳   ✳   ✳

"You said a girl, Dad!"

My thirteen-year-old voice rings with indignation at the skinny, pale-faced boy with thick, dark hair edging into the farmhouse kitchen. He stands, clutching his gas-mask and a battered case, blushing furiously.

92

My father is many things. Cattle man, vet, farm-hand — all the things he's had to be since the able-bodied men in the village have joined up and he's run Wiseacre Farm single-handed.

"Isobel Stewart, this young man's a long way from home and deserves a little courtesy."

Colour floods my face. I'm in trouble and do my best to make amends. I smile. The boy scowls back.

Mum's already clucking over him, like the mother hen she pretends she isn't, pouring soup into a bowl, standing over him whilst he drinks. When he's managed enough to satisfy even her strict dictates, she shows him upstairs to the small back room she says he must make his own. Back downstairs, he's awkward, fuelled on bravado and a lurking fear he's doing his best to hide.

Illustration by Mark Viney.

I'm my mother's daughter, too. I unbend enough to show him round the farm, soon tiring of his monosyllabic answers to my every question, delivered in an accent I've never come across.

"You haven't much to say for yourself," I mutter at last.

"When I've somefing to say, I'll say it!" He fires up angrily, like a small bantam cock.

An inauspicious start. Over the next few days, we circle each other warily. I don't want him here; he so patently doesn't want to be here. So why has he come?

"Give the lad time. It's bound to take a while," I hear Mum say.

It takes all the evacuees in our village a while, the problem being no-one seems to want them. Perhaps that's the start of me and Jake. It's all right for

93

me to feel put out, but I won't put up with others put out, too. What has it to do with anyone else? We're in the playground and he's circled by a crowd of jeering children.

"Cockney sparrow . . . bet your parents didn't want you, either."

Children are cruel. He's willing to take them on, on the verge of tears, determined not to show it.

"Leave him alone, Jock Tindall!" I snap, picking on the ringleader and stepping in.

For a moment, things could escalate and Jake moves towards me protectively. Fortunately the bell goes and everyone sees sense and drifts away. Jake smiles a slow, loping grin that transforms his face.

"I'll walk home with you after, if you like," he mutters sheepishly.

"OK." I shrug, oddly pleased, pretending not to care one way or another.

Things have changed. Me and Jake against the rest, whoever they might be. I've always had a rebellious streak and it turns out Jake has, too. We walk home together and back the following morning. He carries my bag and at night, when we return, we sit at the table together to do our homework.

MORE days pass. Starting to find his feet, he offers to help with the chores around the farm.

"Make him feel at home, love." My mum nods encouragingly. I don't need to be told and shoot her a reproachful glance. Together we feed the hens, turn the butter, lug the buckets of swill for Dolores, the black spot pig who's just farrowed nine curly-tailed piglets. Jake leans over the sty, scratching her back and laughing at the way her giant hanks quiver.

"I could like living here," he admits quietly.

I could like having him here, I decide. Mum, humming happily, makes supper, pushing a plate of scones our way in the meantime, just to keep us going. There's no place for rationing on a farm. Life goes on pretty much the same irrespective of any war.

One day, to my surprise, Jake's mother turns up, a thin woman with sad eyes who sits nursing her teacup and toying with the cake my mother insists she has. She doesn't want it. She's come to see how Jake's fixed and I can see she's pleased. He's pleased, too, trying hard not to show it.

I think how much he must miss her and what it must feel like being so far from home amongst strangers, no matter how welcoming. He pulls away when she hugs him, though his eyes, dark like hers, never leave her face. When she's gone,

relieved to find him so settled, he goes for a walk on his own, refusing my company. I'm piqued.

"All right?" I ask carelessly when he returns. I don't like to see him upset.

"Of course he is," Mum interjects, piling his plate high as if she thinks somehow this might compensate. My parents don't always say much, but neither do they miss much. I guess they know the way he's feeling. Jake's a part of the family now, whether he likes it or not. The brother I never had, the son my parents couldn't have. Mum's always said I couldn't be bettered, but now I wonder if they might have liked more children about the place.

SPRING becomes summer too quickly. Where has all this time gone? Jake's mother doesn't visit again, but she writes short newsy letters which upset him more than anything. His life has somehow merged into mine and neither of us can do without the other. After school, after homework and chores, the time is ours.

In the dying heat of the long, hot summer we roam the hills, climb trees, paddle in the brook after tiddlers, wandering home only as the sun sets. We take no heed of the scoldings our lateness provokes, and stay out late the next night, too, to the despair of my mother.

The war is gathering pace, the Allied forces pushing Hitler back so the talk now is of how long he can hold out. Jake's filling out, shooting up and past me, and has started calling me "Shorty".

In a few short weeks, we're reading avidly about the D-Day landings, tracking the advance into Paris on a map rolled out on the kitchen table. We're winning the war and I should be ecstatic, but something strikes me then that I can hardly bear to think.

"You'll go home," I announce suddenly, the truth dawning.

"Suppose," he mutters, frowning, his eyes locking on to mine as if he's only just realised it, too. He feels the same about the farm as I do. We love it. It's a part of us. We're subdued for a day or so but it doesn't last as there's too much else to occupy us. Life on the farm goes on. We're growing up.

It's Christmas and, as usual, Mum's gone overboard. The place is groaning with food and any neighbour is welcome. Jake and I go up to the wood at the back of the farm to fetch some holly. We're fifteen, not exactly children, though neither are we adult yet. Betwixt and between, Mum says, and it explains why we're as awkward as we are.

"You're so lucky, Issy," Jake mutters, peering through a gap in the trees to fields like patchwork sprinkled with snowfall. Beyond lies the farmhouse rimed with frost and sparkling in the bright sunshine. I am lucky, though I've never given it credence before.

Jake's seen something high up in one of the trees. Agile, he shins up, dropping nimbly to his feet to hold a strand of mistletoe above my head. He's grinning from ear to ear, so I'm not sure I oughtn't to slap him. But then his smile disappears and so does mine, causing my heart to lurch.

I lean over to kiss his cheek, horrified to find his lips instead. They taste of warm days and springtime, and I don't understand the sensation it provokes nor why, when finally we pull away, we're both so flame-faced and can't look at one another.

Jake watches me.

"We ought not to do that again."

I'm certain we shouldn't. Unaccountably tongue-tied I nod, sensing this is serious grown-up stuff neither of us is ready for.

Over the next few days, we don't deliberately avoid each other, yet neither do we seek each other out.

"All right, my love?" Mum murmurs, frowning in a way suggesting she guesses something's not. Jake's out with Dad and the herd up in the meadows, a thing he's taken to doing of late, like he's taken to hanging around with the boys from school instead of me, discussing what they'll do when finally they leave.

"Things are confusing," I mutter, staring down at my plate, unhappy that I can't explain the way I feel. Mum smiles and pats my cheek.

"You're growing up. Confusion happens."

THE winter's been mild, fast sliding into spring. Buds are swelling, trees groaning with foliage, the swallows' nests under the eaves already warmed with clusters of bright eggs.

The Russians are on the outskirts of Berlin, and Jake has a visitor.

"Mother!" he cries, face beaming when he bursts into the kitchen. Momentarily overcome, he stands, grinning idiotically before folding her into his arms. She can't believe how much he's grown. She's wiping tears away.

If possible, Jake's mother is thinner and greyer, and I'm grown up enough now to know her war's been a hard one. We've all read the papers. We know how bad the bombing's been. After lunch, she spends time closeted in the sitting-room with Mum. What's transpired is revealed when they emerge. Jake is to stay on after the war and help Dad around the farm.

Time stands still. Jake's staying? Life swells with a joy I've never known.

"You have a future here, son." Martha Connors refuses his protests, which are immediate. Doesn't he want to stay? How could he bear to leave me? And yet I sense there's nothing his mother wants more than to take him home with her.

Love is complex, but even I never guessed it could be so unselfish.

Jake isn't the only one with important things to consider. After the summer holidays, I'm to start secretarial college in Hutton. The arrangement suits. I'm restless, clinging to the familiar, yet wanting change. But how can I tell if Jake feels about me as I feel about him, if neither of us has the courage to talk of it?

Children's Classics

"Black Beauty"
by Anna Sewell.

THIS perennial children's classic, published on November 24, 1877, was never actually intended for children at all — Anna Sewell's envisaged audience was people who worked with horses.

Anna's passion for horses began early in her life, as did her introduction to writing — she is said to have helped edit some of her mother's works. The combination was a success — Anna broke new literary ground by writing, for the first time, a novel from a horse's point of view, to high critical acclaim.

"Black Beauty" was Anna's debut novel, written late in life, only months before her death. She did live long enough to see it become a near-instant hit, and the book went on to sell more than fifty million copies. It remains one of the best-selling books of all time.

"Black Beauty" was quite different from many of the overtly moralistic stories popular in its era, and it was very much concerned with animal welfare and bringing to light inhumane practice. The book has even been credited with helping to cease the cruel use of the bearing rein, popular in Victorian times, and with improvements in the working practices and conditions among London horse-drawn taxicab drivers.

But the real and lasting draw of the book is Anna's fantastic characterisations of the horses who make up the story — Black Beauty, Duchess, Rob Roy, Ginger, Rory and Lizzie, amongst many others.

"Black Beauty" has remained popular for over one hundred and thirty years, inspiring other writers to compose stories based on Black Beauty's relatives, a sequel, and even a Spike Milligan parody.

Anna Sewell's popularity and place in British literary history is cemented with every new child who discovers the delight of "Black Beauty", and both author and story are very fondly remembered. Indeed, in 2006 a first edition copy of "Black Beauty", dedicated by the author to her mother, sold for £33,000 at auction in London. ∎

"You're quiet," he mutters, taking a glass of the lemonade I've brought up to Top Acre. They're gathering the harvest. August has been hot, burnishing the corn heads with gold. Dad's driving the plough, Jake raking the stooks and heaving them up on to the wagon.

"I'm just busy," I admit.

"I miss you," he says, proffering his empty glass so our fingertips touch, sending shivers running the length of my spine. He grins and I know he's done it on purpose. Why deny what we both know exists?

The postman's cycling down the path towards the farmhouse and suddenly I've pushed the tray of drinks into his hands and am running crazily back down the meadow. Jake stares after me, shaking his head.

There's a letter by the kitchen door and it's not the college prospectus I'm expecting, but a letter for Jake with a London postmark. I pick it up and turn it over. Sensing something serious, I weigh it in my hand before taking it back outside and up to Jake. He throws down his pitchfork and rips it open, quickly scanning the single sheet of paper.

"Mother's ill." He looks up quickly, his troubled gaze meeting mine. He stuffs the letter in his pocket and runs back to the farm. I tell Dad, then Mum, find train times and offer to drive him to the station in the cart. The only London train of the day leaves in an hour. There is no time to waste, no time to think what effect this will have on what we thought cast in stone. In too short a time I'm standing on the platform, looking up as he leans from the carriage window, wondering how we got to this point.

"Let me know when you get there."

"I'll write . . ."

"Jake, will you come back?"

The thought springs into my head and out of my mouth. Why wouldn't he want to come back? The train's already moving. I'm walking, running, struggling to keep pace.

"I'll be back as soon as I can, Issy!" he cries. "You do know I . . ." The whistle blows, drowning his words. I shout that I love him, too.

The train's disappeared and I know I can't stand there for ever.

FRUSTRATED days follow. I write to Jake, desperate for an answer that never arrives, no matter how I rush downstairs at the first sound of the postman.

"Someone should have gone with him," Mum scolds, glaring at Dad as if she thinks it's his fault.

"He'll send word if he needs us," is Dad's advice.

As much as we want him, Jake isn't a part of this family — Jake has family of his own.

At long last, the eagerly anticipated letter arrives. I rip it open, disappointed in the few scribbled lines written in obvious haste. Martha Connors has pneumonia. She won't go into hospital and the most he can do is to get her to stay in bed. No word of if he's missing me. Mum chides me gently. How can I be so selfish as to think he'd have time for me? She's right, of course, but is he really so busy he can't give me a single thought?

Life regains some semblance of normality. I start college. I help out at home and write to Jake again, filling him in on the news and adding that I'll come and see him if he'd like. Two agonising weeks follow in which there's no letter.

"This has gone on long enough," Mum decides. "One of us will have to go."

"Happen you're right," Dad says, more worried than he's letting on.

"Let me," I suggest quietly, refusing to listen to the instant protests.

It makes sense. Single-handed, Dad has too much on with the farm, and it's hard for Mum to leave him. As much as they love Jake, I love him more. I can't sleep. I can't eat. All I know is I have to see him. My love can conquer anything if only I know for certain Jake loves me, too.

I T'S autumn now and it's damp and dark. I've disembarked at Paddington, unprepared for the desolation of buildings reduced to rubble. Sobered, I find a cab and drive down back streets, turning off at last towards grim terraces next to a warehouse miraculously untouched. We pull up. In a voice reminiscent of Jake's, the cab driver informs me cheerfully that I have reached my destination. I pay him and scramble out, hesitating before knocking on the door of the house in the middle of the row. The door drags open. My heart leaps with a life of its own.

"Issy?" For a moment, Jake can't disguise his happiness.

It doesn't last.

"What are you doing here?" he demands, sounding cross.

Why does he feel the need to ask?

"We've been so worried," I stumble out.

"Who is it, Jake?" Martha Connors's voice floats past him, frail and weak.

There's nothing else he can do but ask me into the dark hallway, to a small back room which passes for kitchen and sitting-room both.

He's done what he can. The room's tidy and passably clean, the invalid huddled in a chair by the fire, flushing with pleasure to see who it is. Whilst

Jake makes tea, she tells me all that's happened and that Jake won't leave her, no matter how she's begged him. I pass on the last thing Mum said before I got on the train.

"Tell Martha she must come to the farm for a holiday." Will she come? I'm desperate she should say yes.

"We'd all love to have you," I implore, seeing her hesitate, yet sensing how much she wants to. She darts a quick, nervous glance towards Jake, who only snorts.

Why is he behaving like this? I don't understand.

"We'll go for a walk," he says abruptly as soon as I've finished my tea.

OUTSIDE, alone together, there's so much I want to say.

"You must bring her, Jake. Please tell me you will."

"When she's well enough," he mutters, staring straight ahead. He walks with long loping strides through the grim, shuttered streets. I struggle to keep up.

"Why didn't you write?" I burst out, unable to keep it in any longer.

Thankfully he stops, giving me a chance to catch up, his gaze taking in the broken skyline around. He can't believe I've asked.

"I'd no idea what I'd find when I got here," he says, swallowing hard. "I never realised what she'd been through. On her own, with no-one to turn to. All the while making sure I was . . ."

"Safe and sound?" I interject, beginning to understand. He's full of guilt. He thinks he should have known. "Jake, it's not your fault! You were a child, doing what you were told. It wasn't easy coming to live amongst strangers . . ."

"Never strangers, Issy!" He gazes down into my eyes and at last he's Jake again. A troubled Jake, acknowledging the feeling between us even he can't deny. "The farm seems a dream," he whispers. "And best to leave it that way. I can't abandon her a second time. Holiday or not, this is my life now."

I smile and reach for his hand, feeling it clasp, strong and gentle, around my own.

Is this the time to mention the tumble-down cottage, scene of our childhood games on the edge of our estate, wanting only hard work to do it up? Plenty of room for Jake and Martha, Dad has suggested hopefully. A place for me, too, when I've finished college and found a job.

I'm going too fast and need to slow down. My heart beats wildly, full of feelings I long to express and know this isn't the time for.

"We need to talk. Come for a holiday first. See Mum and Dad," I murmur, reaching up and gently kissing him.

He kisses me back. Does he guess I have a solution to this mess? He grins. I grin back. Whatever happens, whatever decisions we reach, our love is strong. And there, in the background, lacing our lives, is the farm, permanent and unchangeable. ■

A Chance For Thomas

Illustration by David Axtell.

THE headmaster had sent for Nellie.

"I have news for you, Miss Baker," he told her.

Nellie had been putting the children through their paces, listening to them recite their seven-times multiplication table, and was none too pleased at the interruption.

As she stood in the headmaster's sparse office, she tried to quell the

by Lorna Howarth.

feeling of anxiety in the pit of her stomach. Mr Percival's large, pale eyes stared at her as she twisted the thick brown serge of her skirt between her fingers. Oh, dear. Was she in trouble again?

"I have decided," Mr Percival said at last, "that I am going to relinquish the reins of responsibility for the Empire Day celebrations this year."

Is that it, Nellie thought. He wasn't calling her along to his office for a row after all. She had almost breathed a sigh of relief when he suddenly spoke again.

"Now, *you* are going to do it!"

"Me, sir?"

How could that be? She had only been at Mayberry School for seven months and it was her first appointment. How would she go about such a thing? Mayberry's might only be a small school, but she knew that people would flock from miles around to celebrate Empire Day. She wasn't ready for that sort of responsibility!

Mr Percival raised his thick grey eyebrows at her.

"Do I take it that you are not pleased, Miss Baker? I fail to understand why that might be so. You are a qualified teacher, are you not?"

"Yes, sir, of course I am."

But not a very experienced one, she added to herself. Even from the time of her interview, she had felt that Mr Percival had not liked her very much. Perhaps this was some kind of test. Perhaps he was expecting her to say no, and he would use that as an excuse not to keep her on?

Well, she would just have to do her very best then, wouldn't she? Her parents had made too many sacrifices to put her through college for her to give up easily. She wasn't going to let them — or herself — down!

A WEEK later, Nellie stepped down from her raised desk and stood facing her class.

"Now, then, children! As you know, Empire Day is only just over a month away. We are going to do something different this year." She reached out and rapped with her ruler on her desk, cutting through the murmurings of excitement that had erupted.

"We will still march up to the church as usual, but only for prayers, and then we will come straight back to school afterwards. We are going to perform a pageant! Outside in the playing area if the weather is fine, indoors if it is not."

A shaft of spring sunshine fell through the high windows, across the jar of daffodils on the nature table and on to the black stove in the corner of the classroom. Forty-three pairs of eyes stared at her intently. If only they paid as much attention to their arithmetic lessons!

"And now for the really exciting part. Class Two, our class, children, is going to put on a play!"

There was a collective intake of breath and Nellie pressed on.

"Each of the countries of our Empire will be represented by a child in national dress, who will also carry a symbol of that country. For example, if Eunice was chosen to represent India, she could wear a sari, or if Reginald were to represent New Zealand, he could carry a toy lamb or some wool. We will be discussing all that later.

"We will also make flags and each of you will write an invitation to your parents, asking them if they would like to attend. School will close for a holiday in the afternoon, of course."

She smiled as a whoop of excitement went round the class. Nellie had chosen the last lesson of the afternoon to break the news, as she knew that the children would be too excited to get much work done after her announcement.

"Shh, now! We don't want to disturb Mr Percival."

The headmaster took Class Three on Tuesday and Thursday afternoons for composition and the folding doors that divided the two classrooms were flimsy. She'd been taken to task once this week already for the amount of noise she allowed her class to make.

She'd tried to explain that she thought children learned so much better if they were allowed to enjoy themselves, but Mr Percival certainly didn't share her views.

"Enjoy?" He had almost bellowed the words. "Enjoy? What unorthodox notions you have, Miss Baker! The children are not here to enjoy themselves. They are here to learn. Two distinctly different objectives!"

NELLIE'S thoughts were brought back by the movement of a hand shooting up.

"Can I be New Zealand, miss?" It was Dottie Maddock. Dottie, like young Thomas Thorn, was always amongst the first to volunteer.

Right on cue, Thomas raised his hand, too.

"That ain't fair, miss. She always gets chosen for the best things."

"Isn't fair, Thomas," Nellie corrected. "But all that will be decided later. I will put forward recommendations, but it's Mr Percival who will make the final decisions."

She walked across the classroom, her steps echoing on the bare, unpolished boards, and stopped at the easel. She divided the blackboard into columns with her piece of chalk, heading each with the vacant parts to be filled.

"Anyone wishing to be considered please write your names clearly, in your best handwriting, mind. After all, we want Mr Percival to see how it's improving, don't we? In an orderly fashion, please. Row one first. Lead on, Thomas."

"Yes, miss." Stocky little Thomas Thorn stalked up to the blackboard, his copper curls bouncing gently on top of his head, and stood on tiptoe to scratch his name with a piece of chalk. His normally wide grin disappeared as he concentrated on spelling his name out in the column headed *Australia*.

"I've writ me name as high as I can, miss, so's there's room for other people underneath."

"Thank you, Thomas. But it's written, Thomas. I have written my name."

"Have yer, miss? I thought it were just fer us kids." He laughed and Nellie quickly turned away to stop herself from laughing, too. Thomas had an irrepressible sense of humour, but she knew that, if Mr Percival heard, he would be punished for insubordination.

Sometimes she felt that she was the only one to recognise Thomas's quick and able mind in his cheeky sallies. If only that wit were more readily present in his written work, he'd be top of the class. Her heart went out to him because, however hard he tried, he was always at the bottom.

A S soon as the last volunteer, Phyllis Smith, had written her name, the school bell sounded. But, for once, the children hung back, reluctant to escape and eager to know more.

"Class Three are forming a choir to lead the singing and Class

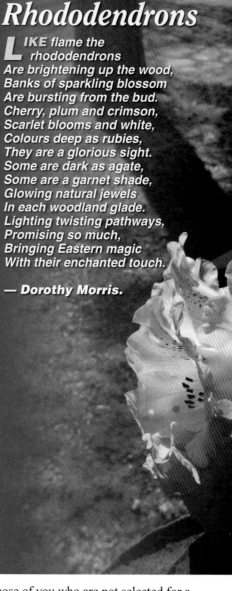

Rhododendrons

L IKE flame the rhododendrons
Are brightening up the wood,
Banks of sparkling blossom
Are bursting from the bud.
Cherry, plum and crimson,
Scarlet blooms and white,
Colours deep as rubies,
They are a glorious sight.
Some are dark as agate,
Some are a garnet shade,
Glowing natural jewels
In each woodland glade.
Lighting twisting pathways,
Promising so much,
Bringing Eastern magic
With their enchanted touch.

— Dorothy Morris.

One will provide a dancing display. Those of you who are not selected for a major role must not worry. There will be lots of other duties to perform, like carrying the flags and such. It will be wonderful fun."

After the children had at last filed out, Nellie walked up to the blackboard and took stock of her volunteers. Most of the names, unsurprisingly, were in the column headed *Britannia*, the key part in the play. She would have to put the names in a hat for each part. It must be fair, after all.

Under Mr Percival's eagle eye, the draw was made and Nellie was delighted when Thomas's name was drawn for Australia. Mr Percival, however, was far from delighted.

"A boy who regularly comes at the bottom of the class should not be rewarded in such a way," he declared sternly.

Despite the unease she always felt in her headmaster's presence, Nellie could not stop her retort.

"His lack of academic achievement is not his fault, sir, I'm quite sure of that. Thomas works very hard at his lessons."

Mr Percival gave Nellie one of his stony stares and made her wait a full minute before answering.

"I can see I was right about your unorthodox ideas, Miss Baker, but, seeing as I put you in charge, I suppose I must allow it this time."

Thomas had been delighted, of course, and had even come up with the suggestion that he carry a basket of apples as a symbol of Australia's productivity. But, as Nellie had feared, he found learning his speech difficult. Then she had the idea of getting him to recite it after her and he soon had the whole thing off pat. It was making sense of things on paper that was so difficult for him.

Excitement grew as the great day approached. Nellie used the lessons usually reserved for "drill" to teach the children their speeches and movements, and it wasn't long before they were taking their places and pronouncing their lines with fewer and fewer mistakes.

"It's a good job it's me doing Australia, miss," Thomas told her when he saw the basket of apples at the dress rehearsal. "I'm the strongest one in the class and I can easily lift that lot."

He raised his arm to flex his muscles.

"It's 'cos I help me dad out on the farm."

AND so, with everything going well with the rehearsals and the day fast approaching, Nellie began to congratulate herself. Everything seemed to be going really well.

However, her confidence proved to be premature. For, on the very day before Empire Day itself, Thomas's place in the front row was empty!

Nellie stared at the gap in the row of children. It stared back at her, obvious as a missing tooth.

"Do any of you know why Thomas is absent?" she asked anxiously, looking up from her register.

A hand went up in the middle row.

"Hester? You have some information?"

"Yes, miss." Hester flicked her fair plaits over her shoulder, lifting her chin importantly. "Chalky White as works on Thomas's farm has broken his leg, miss, and Thomas 'as to stay at home to help."

"It's true, miss," Ned Williams chipped in. "Chalky White lives down our lane and we seen him being carted orf to 'ospital."

"Dear, oh, dear," Nellie exclaimed, forgetting to correct his grammar as the news sank in. But it wasn't the fact that poor Chalky White was ill that was making her heart flip. She wished him well, of course she did. No, it was the fact that she was now missing a country from her play.

What was she going to do? She had only asked the children to learn their own lines. How stupid she had been. She had not thought to give the major parts an understudy.

Her pulse raced. It was all going to be a failure, she was sure it was. She couldn't leave out a whole country from the Empire, could she? Mr Percival would spot it straight away. She could just picture him in the front row watching the performance, a frown of disapproval on his face. He would dismiss her for sure, she just knew he would!

All day the problem whirled in her head. She could get one of the children who didn't have a major part to stand in, of course, but how would they ever learn the lines in time? Perhaps one of them could just read the lines? It would look bad, but what else could she do at such short notice?

By the time the school bell clanged out its home-time rhythm she could feel a headache beginning. She dismissed the children with a final reminder to them to be bright and early for the morrow and turned to clean the blackboard of the day's work.

It was as she was rubbing with the cloth, trying not to breathe in the flurry of chalk dust that swirled around her, that she had her idea.

Of course! Why hadn't she thought of it before?

That evening, Nellie found herself outside the door of the Thorns' farmhouse. She pulled herself up to her full five foot three as she entered the little porch, stepping past a row of geraniums that stood in pots on the floor.

As she waited after knocking on the faded blue door Nellie recalled the local talk about how Mr Thorn was working all hours to make a go of the farm he had recently inherited from his father. She knew only too well how hard it could be suddenly to be in charge of things and now, with Chalky White out of action, it must be even more difficult for him.

She was just lifting the knocker to knock again when the door opened. Mrs Thorn was wearing a long print apron wrapped around her dress and her cheeks were flushed. She stood there, wiping flour from her hands.

"Oh, it's you, Miss Baker," she said and sighed. "If you're here to complain about our Tom not bein' at school, you needn't bother, 'cos there's nothing I can do about it. Our Arthur's said he's got to stay off and that's all there is to it."

"Please, Mrs Thorn, I won't keep you a moment. Will you hear me out?"

Mrs Thorn reluctantly opened the door further and allowed her into the warm farmhouse kitchen.

After she had listened to Miss Baker's suggestion she sat back and smiled in relief.

"Well, well, Miss Baker, that's a novel idea! You must want our Tom bad if you be prepared to do that." Her eyes lit up with humour. "I'll have to check with my Arthur, of course, but I don't see as he'll mind too much."

✳   ✳   ✳   ✳

The twenty-fourth of May, Empire Day, dawned fair and bright. The sun shone in a clear blue sky as Nellie lined up her class in pairs and marched them with the other classes to St Peter's Church at the end of the lane. In the dark echoing church they recited the Lord's Prayer, received a blessing from the vicar and then returned down the lane to school for the pageant.

Whilst they had been at church, a large group of parents had gathered on the playing area at the back of the school. They were mostly mothers, of course, but there were a few caps to be seen, too, dotted here and there.

When everyone was in position, the children stood in line to salute the Union Flag. Then Class Three led the singing and they all joined in "Jerusalem" and "God Save The King" and then "Land Of Hope And Glory". Mr Percival gave a compelling, inspirational speech and told them a tale about Clive of India who was a great hero.

Then came Nellie's play. Thomas carried his basket with great pride, beaming at everyone, his head held high with importance. He didn't forget a single word of his lines.

Even Mr Percival, gaunt and regal in his best suit and starched white collar, smiled and applauded with the rest when the celebrations were finished. The children stood in rows, the boys proudly taking their bows and the girls, long hair tied back with white ribbons, bobbing the curtseys they had practised.

"Well done, Miss Baker!" Mr Percival said afterwards, when the parents and children had gone home.

"Thank you, headmaster."

"I'll have to make sure I give you the task of organising things again next year, seeing as how you have made such a success of it."

His words sent a glow of happiness through Nellie. But it wasn't just the praise that sent her pulses racing. It was the mention of next year. Her heart soared. That meant that he was keeping her on. Just wait until she told her mother and her father the news!

However, she thought, quickly coming back down to earth, there was a price to be paid first!

ANKLE deep in muck and with loud mooing filling her ears, Nellie paused and leaned for a moment on the spade Mr Thorn had provided her with and looked across the farmyard. A swallow dived out from beneath the cow shed roof and swept low across the yard, its blue-black back and smart orange bib glinting in the evening sunshine.

She caught Thomas's father's eye as he paused at the gate and turned to look across at her, disbelief written across his face. She smiled at him and then went back to the pile of cow manure she had cleared, glancing over at the mess she still had to shovel away.

But nothing, not the mess nor the smell, not even the ache that was beginning in her back, could stop the happiness she felt. She breathed out a long, contented sigh.

Unorthodox, Mr Percival had called her, hadn't he? Well, she supposed it was unorthodox to have taken over some of Thomas's chores in return for his attendance, but if anyone asked her, she would tell them.

It had definitely been worth it! ■

No Place Like Home

J O rubbed her head where she'd bumped it yet again on the sloping ceiling of the tiny porch, and wondered why she'd ever thought her little house's quirks were so endearing.

Its solid stone walls were permanently cold to the touch. With small, old-fashioned windows, it always seemed dark inside. And the porch where she kept her sturdy waterproofs and walking boots still caught her out, as it had just now, even after two years.

The boots and waterproofs were essential to anyone living round here, of

by Rebecca Holmes.

Illustration by
Gerard Fay.

109

course, and had been part of her life, in various sizes and colours, for as long as she could remember.

Her father, a keen walker, had always made a point of living no more than an hour's drive away from the Lake District. As soon as Jo had been old enough to accompany him, he'd introduced her to the gentler routes, gradually progressing to the more challenging fells.

Not surprisingly, she'd grown up to love the place as much as he did. So when a suitable job had come up in the area, she'd jumped at the chance.

"What if you feel different after a while?" her friend, Melissa, warned. "You might find you're stuck all the way out there."

But Jo hankered for the wide-open spaces and ever-changing nature of the mountains. When a great-aunt left her a useful legacy, and her parents had also been willing to help out towards a deposit on a terraced house, she'd reckoned the omens were pointing in one direction, and that was the direction she took.

Now, though, she found even beautiful surroundings could lose their charm when she ended up in traffic jams at tourist bottlenecks on her way home from work, often with her car's windscreen wipers going at full pelt. Goodness only knew where Wordsworth had got his idea about wandering lonely as a cloud. Clouds always had plenty of company so far as she could see — each other!

It was different from the days when she'd shared a house with her old university friends. There would always be someone to talk to, or go out to the theatre or cinema with. Here, she hardly seemed to know anyone her own age. Perhaps the time was right to move back to the Smoke, admit that the Lake District was just for holidays.

"It's up to you," her dad said when she phoned him. "Personally speaking, if I'd ever moved to the Lakes, wild horses wouldn't drag me away, but reality can be different from the dream. Just remember, though — if you do go back, you won't be able to change your mind."

※　※　※　※

It was the fourth morning in a row that Melissa hadn't been able to get a seat on the bus. To add insult to injury, the bus company had just announced another fare increase.

Not that she should be complaining, she supposed. She had a job slap-bang in the centre of the very same city where she had so enjoyed being a student. Wasn't that what she'd always aimed for?

Coming from a small backwater in the middle of nowhere, Melissa had dreamed of city lights and glamour. Getting into university here had been a major step in making that dream come true.

She loved the big name department stores, with masses of space devoted to her favourite cosmetics, and assistants practically queuing up to offer free makeovers. The only drawback was that she was always tempted to buy some of the products afterwards, and they cost more than she could afford.

In true Melissa style, though, she had soon overcome that hurdle by getting a part-time job on one of the counters she'd enjoyed frequenting. To her astonishment, after finishing her degree, she'd been taken on as a management trainee at the same store.

"Your experience and enthusiasm shone through," she was told later.

Melissa didn't feel so enthusiastic now, swept along by the stream of commuters all heading for their allotted buildings. The tall glass and concrete towers looked dismal in the never-ending rain. The best word to describe the appearance of the old cathedral, which usually stood so proud, was "dispirited". Even the fountains in the adjoining square were a dull, uniform grey, with no sunlight to sparkle through them and make rainbows.

"Practically everywhere looks miserable in this weather," Helen, her boss, said over coffee during their break. "If you'd done what your family expected, right now you'd be teaching in a classroom full of damp children." She put on a mock-thoughtful expression. "Aroma of damp clothes, or the latest fragrance from Chanel? Difficult choice."

Melissa laughed, yet she still felt restless. Who'd have thought she would grow bored with city life? While it used to be fun sharing a house with friends, there had been changes over the last couple of years. Jo had left, for instance, even though everyone had said she was mad at the time.

Lately, she'd taken to reading lifestyle magazines instead of her usual fashion glossies. She liked looking through them last thing at night, in bed with cup of tea. Along with the features on how people had renovated cosy cottages with various "finds", her favourite sections were those interviewing women who had set up their own businesses. Home-made scented soaps and oils featured frequently. So far as Melissa could gather, they didn't seem that difficult to make, and with her sales and marketing training . . .

It would be a huge gamble, and she'd still need a job to support herself. Still, it was worth doing some research. Jo had taken the plunge. She might have some good advice.

JUST over a hundred miles away, Jo was sitting by her fireplace, flicking through a fashion magazine she had picked up on a whim in the small local supermarket. She couldn't remember when she'd last bought one of these. It made her quite nostalgic for former days when she and Melissa used to go round the city centre shops together. Of course, Mel was still there and, knowing her, still shopping till she dropped. Perhaps she was the best person to help her arrive at a decision.

✳   ✳   ✳   ✳

"Well, well, well. So the wanderer returns! What happened? Sheep suddenly stop talking to you?"

"Very funny, Richard. I see your so-called sense of humour hasn't changed much, then."

"Oh, that hurt." Richard put a hand to his heart.

Jo smiled as she picked up her case and headed for the stairs. It had been an inspired decision of Mel's for them to try a "house swap" for a few days to help them work out what they really wanted. It felt strange coming back, though, and she was glad that at least one of the original housemates was still in residence.

"Mel still has the same room," Richard said. "Up in the sky. You might need an oxygen mask. I'm afraid someone else rents your old room. We don't see her much. She works nights."

"Yes, Mel told me. Fancy a drink later?"

"I would, but I've got an early start at work — which means setting off even earlier to beat the rush hour. It's not just you country folk who get up at the crack of dawn, you know."

Jo swallowed her disappointment and managed a grin.

"An early night would probably do me good. I'd forgotten how busy the motorway gets the further south you come. And I intend to put in a full day tomorrow."

Later, just before she settled down for the night, Jo opened the attic window to gaze out at the lights stretching to the horizon and listened to the hum of the traffic.

"The city never sleeps," she murmured to herself. "But I'm going to."

As she crawled under the duvet and settled down, she thought dreamily of all the life going on outside.

※ ※ ※ ※

To be honest, when Jo's neighbour, Marie, showed her in, Melissa realised she'd been expecting something more quaint. Something like the restful sound of a nearby stream fresh from the mountains, perhaps.

"There's a handy little supermarket just round the corner," Marie said, breaking into her thoughts. "And Jo told me she's left the fridge well stocked."

A fridge that didn't have to be shared? Wonderful!

"Then there are some spare blankets in the cupboard if you need them. It can get cold here at night. Now, do let me know if there's anything you need. I'm only next door."

Later that evening, Melissa could hardly believe how time had flown. She'd been so comfortable sitting by a proper fireplace in a proper little sitting-room. After a while she'd even switched off the television and listened to the ticking of the clock.

"Well," she said to the stillness, "I suppose I'd better turn in. I've got a long day ahead tomorrow if I want to do all the things I've been planning."

Upstairs, she parted the curtains and looked outside. Beyond the edge of the little town, everything was a dark, dark blue, almost black.

Wow, she thought. All that empty space!

"So, how is the big, bad city?" Melissa asked on the phone the following evening.

"Great," Jo answered. "Or it was, once I'd battled my way in and managed to find a space in that massive multi-storey car park!"

"If you think that's bad, you should try the public transport. It's like playing sardines, without the party. But tell me about the rest."

"Oh, Mel, I'd forgotten what it was like to go round a warm, comfortable shopping centre and still have more to see at the end of it. I even treated myself to some new clothes. And I've booked a ticket for a play tonight. It's got the lead actor from that series we were talking about. I suppose you've already seen it?"

"To be honest, I haven't been keeping up with these things recently," Melissa admitted. "But if he's in it, I'll definitely check it out. Anyway, my day was very revealing," she continued, and went on to describe how, after picking up the hire car, she'd visited one of the local market towns, plus a couple of villages, exploring craft and gift shops.

"Obviously, they prefer local products, but if I could make soaps and candles infused with blended aromatherapy oils, and labelled with their specific properties — calming, uplifting and so on — I bet there'd be a gap in the market."

"Hmm," Jo said. "If you want to part customers from their money, I suspect you'll need a Lakeland theme. 'Coniston Calm', perhaps? Or 'Windermere Wonder'? I wouldn't really know, though. I seem to spend all my time sorting out claims for farmers losing their tractors down ditches, or walkers dropping their mobile phones down scree slopes."

"Well, I'm pretty sure I know." Melissa couldn't help feeling slightly nettled at what she saw as her friend's lukewarm response. "Maybe it's the freshness of the air up here, but I've got a good feeling about this. Tomorrow I'll go round the gift shops in poets' houses and visitor centres to check out the opportunities there."

Both went quiet for a moment, as if they'd run out of things to say.

True to form, Melissa was the first to restart the conversation. That had always been the trouble with Jo, she thought — the girl had a tendency to sit back and ruminate.

"What are your plans for the next two days?"

"Well, I noticed a massive branch of my favourite chain of bookstores, so I'll happily lose myself in there for a few hours. Then there are a couple of art galleries I'd like to visit. All in all, it looks as if we're both in for a busy time."

THAT was true, yet not quite in the way either of them had expected. Jo felt deliciously self-indulgent as she browsed through books in the plush interior of what had always been her favourite bookshop. She enjoyed the theatre trip, too. In fact, there was a whole range of films and plays available for her to see, not to mention one of her favourite groups performing at a big local venue.

But it would have been so much nicer if there'd been someone to go with. Everyone in the house always seemed to be either on their way out or just coming in and about to collapse into their rooms. At home, the neighbours were always ready to chat, as were the farmers she saw in her job working for an insurance company. Granted, they usually grumbled about everything, and insisted on serving her mugs of tea strong enough to stand a spoon in, as her dad would say, but they were friendly.

Then there were the shops themselves. At first she'd been impressed by the huge range on offer, and treated herself to a few things she'd been saving for, but a lot of the clothes just weren't practical. And everywhere was crowded.

At least she found one of the art galleries she wanted to visit. The moment she walked into its hushed stillness, she finally found a sense of calm. Not the same calm as the fells and valleys, sadly, but calm nevertheless.

As if by some twist of fate, she came upon a painting of a scene she knew and loved — the Langdale Pikes, as seen across Windermere. Their craggy outlines seemed to look back at her so like old friends, their pull on her was almost physical.

✳   ✳   ✳   ✳

"No wonder there are so many poets and thinkers in the Lakes," Melissa joked a couple of days later. "There's nothing else to do round here. I went round the gift shops, but they don't sell much in the way of the products I'm thinking of, apart from the odd few here and there." She sighed.

"I'm beginning to wonder whether that means a gap in the market or lack of demand. Customers seem mainly interested in mint cake and gingerbread. I even ended up buying a fridge magnet of a sheep! Then there's the fact that everywhere's so spread out. Honestly, your petrol bill must be horrendous."

"That's why I've got a small car." Jo laughed. "It's economical, yet feisty enough to tackle the mountain passes."

"Assuming you're crazy enough to want to do that," Melissa retorted. "And those mountains are decidedly creepy at night. You can almost feel them out there in the dark, looming over everything."

"Do you know what you are?" Jo said. "A Johnny Town-mouse."

"What? As in the Beatrix Potter story, where he goes to the country and really hates it? That makes you the other one, who goes to the town. What was his name?"

"Timmie Willie. He's glad to get home — just as I'll be. And it's even set in the Lake District," Jo said. "So I'm Timmie and you're Johnny."

They both giggled.

"We'll have to remind each other of that next time we get itchy feet and start making outrageous plans," Melissa added. "Anyway, I'll definitely be glad to get back to civilisation, even if the buses are crowded. And covered shopping centres where you can stay warm and dry. Bliss!"

It was bliss indeed for Melissa to come home. She heaved a sigh of relief as she stepped off the train. Even the sight of the city skyline as it neared its destination had set her pulse quickening. She paused for a moment to savour the scene of everyone bustling about.

The thought of the Monday morning "crush hour" still filled her with dread, but she was determined to sort that out. It was time she moved out of the house and nearer the centre. It would cost more, even for something hardly bigger than a broom cupboard, but the savings in travelling costs might help make up the difference. She would manage it somehow.

First things first — her number one priority was a latte from her favourite coffee chain; how she'd missed those! Next, a pair of glamorous shoes so she could get changed out of these sensible monstrosities.

As Melissa walked out on to the street, buildings towering above her, she felt well and truly glad to be back.

JO felt her spirits rise even as she drove up the motorway and spotted those same mountains that her friend had complained about, blue in the distance, as if waiting to welcome her.

Of course, she needed more friends of her own age, and it was up to her, she realised now, to make the effort to get out and meet people. She'd already decided to join a walking club, as well as start going to one of the little theatres dotted around the district.

While it was true that the house was cold, there was such a thing as insulation. According to Richard, with whom she had managed some conversation and who apparently knew about these things, she might be able to get a grant to help with the cost.

As for the dark rooms? Nothing a few tins of paint and some lighter-coloured curtains couldn't solve, judging from the tips she'd read in the magazines on Melissa's bedside table. She just had to remember to mind her head on that porch. ■

THE clocks had gone forward and the evenings were getting lighter, yet I still got quite a fright when suddenly I saw him, a shadowy figure standing motionless in the tangle of lilac and green by the village hall door, staring intently through the dusk up at the windows. He was so quiet and still, almost as if he were on another wavelength . . .

There may have been no sound from him, but he obviously heard me as I halted abruptly.

"Hello!" He turned and smiled. "This is the right place for the meeting, isn't it? And the right night?"

I nodded, and then smiled back as I saw that he was holding one of the leaflets we'd distributed about the village, exhorting our fellows residents to *Tell us what to do with it!*

We were the village hall committee and "it" was money we'd acquired to do the hall up — which it badly needed. Its origins are complicated and it wasn't maintained by the local council. Over recent years, its only revenue had been the proceeds from fairs, fêtes and suchlike, and this lack of any proper funding was seriously starting to show.

Money Well Spent

by Val Bonsall.

We'd managed to get a *sort of* grant. We were thrilled, the half-dozen of us who made up the committee, and had publicised the meeting in the hope that the good news would get a few more of the villagers to join us in the running of the hall. During holiday periods and times like that, the committee could be reduced to two of us — we really did need more members.

"Tom Tyler," the stranger said, shaking hands with Geoff, our chairman, who'd now also arrived. "I've just moved into End Lane Cottage. You know, the one at the end of the lane —"

"Would be, wouldn't it?" Geoff offered dryly.

Geoff was a bit gruff at times, but he really did have a heart of gold.

So we trooped through the door — which had seen better days and was a definite contender for our new-found wealth — and into the hall.

A better heating system might be an idea, too, I decided as I considered taking my jacket off, then opted to leave it on! Tom was the only addition to our usual number. But he was made welcome as he joined us round the

Illustration by Stephanie Axtell.

table. Indeed, Elaine, who worked in the post office, seemed absolutely enchanted by him! I had to agree he was rather good-looking, but only gave him my share of Grace's blueberry muffins because I was trying to cut down.

"I noticed something when I was waiting," Tom said, brushing crumbs off his lap. "There's an unevenness in the brickwork round the windows. So presumably —" he broke off to point at the row of tiny slit windows high in the wall opposite "— they were bigger once?"

"Much bigger," Geoff said.

Geoff knew all about the history of the building and he herded us outside so we could all examine the brickwork and see just how huge the original windows had been.

"Let's put them back, as they were," Tom said. "It would be like a wall of glass, really making us a part of the village — connecting us to it. You say you want more people involved —"

It was then that I started thinking that this man was just not on the same planet as us. New windows the size he wanted would mean all the money would be gone in one fell swoop! I was the treasurer, and I'd given the matter a lot of thought and already listed priorities — like getting the place painted, updating the heating, improving the kitchen, which at the moment just about had facilities for making tea but not much more, or, maybe levelling the land to the side so it could be used for cars . . .

I LOOKED at the others, but couldn't read their expressions in the ever-thickening gloom.

By then Tom had wandered over to the patch of land at the side.

"Is this ours?" he asked, excitement in his voice as he leaned over a fenced-off area.

"Yes," I said, "but we try to keep quiet about it."

Trickling down the hillside behind us on to the edge of our land was a stream, which ended in a pool — a pond — near where I was proposing the extra car parking.

We weren't talking water lilies and cute little ducks swimming around. The water was dark and stagnant, choked up with reeds, rushes and the slime of dead leaves and litter that had been blown in. It was like that when we took over the place, and we'd just let it be.

But Tom had other ideas!

"We should get it cleared out," he said when we were back inside. "Think what a wonderful feature it would be! The village hall with its village pond —"

"Think," I interrupted with emphasis, "how *much* it would cost."

Then I softened my voice. His enthusiasm *was* appealing. It was just that his ideas were wholly impractical and over the top.

"What I mean, Tom," I said, laughing, "is that we haven't won the lottery, you know!"

He laughed, too, as did the others.

I thought we were all in agreement, but I still felt oddly troubled as I went home to the opposite end of the lane where Tom had apparently recently taken up residence.

On Sunday, I walked back to the hall to estimate how many cars we could accommodate if we proceeded with the parking spaces. So there I was, pacing about, using the length of my stride to do rough calculations, when I became aware of someone watching me.

It was Tom, once again partly lost in foliage.

"Is this a private game of hopscotch, or can anyone join in?" he asked, stepping forward.

I told him what I was doing and he explained that he was there for the same reason.

"Or what I mean is, I'm here because of our meeting last week, too."

"Oh?"

"Just to . . . assess things," he said mysteriously.

"These ideas of yours, they're great," I said, "but we just haven't got the money."

"Mmm." He shrugged enigmatically, adjusting the camera slung over his shoulder.

"Great," I repeated, adding more firmly, "but just a dream."

"And what's so wrong with dreams, Rose?" he asked, his grey eyes challenging. "Surely you've had dreams?"

I didn't reply.

But, yes, I'd had dreams . . . once.

WE met again in the hall, all of us on the committee — which now included Tom — a couple of weeks later.

I was a little late. My teenage niece had phoned just as I was leaving the house, and she had talked and talked and talked . . .

I suppose I should have been flattered because, according to my sister and brother-in-law, she never tells them anything! But I like to be on time, so I felt a bit flustered when I arrived.

I needn't have worried, though — they hadn't held the meeting up for me. In fact, they were all engrossed with what I soon saw were pen and coloured-ink drawings of how the hall might look with big fancy windows and the pond all cleaned up and enlarged, too.

Tom — who turned out to be an art teacher — had done them.

"Just to illustrate my point," he said with one of his thoughtful smiles.

I searched in my bag and produced the two estimates for the external painting works that I'd sorted out over the past week, and some blurb from a heating contractor.

"This one here's interesting. Economical and —"

But I'm afraid the brochure on the latest in boilers couldn't compete with Tom's handiwork.

He had done a beautiful job, there was no disputing it, with the pictures enlivened with lots of detail, even down to a heron wading daintily in the pond.

Everyone's eyes kept returning to them.

AFTER that, I was away for ten days, visiting an old school friend. We had a terrific time, as usual, but the return journey on the motorway had been awful. I'd so looked forward to getting on to the empty roads around the village, where tiny wild flowers now flecked the waysides like confetti. But then I found myself stuck, for the final few miles of narrow winding road, behind a large and slow-moving agricultural-type truck with what I recognised as the kids from the farm at the crossroads all sitting in the back.

As we crawled along, I noticed our little convoy being joined by several more orthodox-looking vehicles from the various houses just outside the village . . . and all the occupants of the vehicles heading for the village seemed to be dressed in work clothes . . .

The village hall is one of the first things you see when you enter the village, but that day, all I initially took in was the mass of people milling about around it.

I parked my car — where I could, for there were far more about than usual — and followed the farm family to see what was going on.

Grace greeted me immediately, but this time clutching a tin of paint and a brush rather than her more customary blueberry muffins.

"We're doing the place up ourselves," she announced, "so the grant will go further with no decorators and plumbers and people to pay and we'll be able to afford the windows and the pond."

"Good to see so many people here, isn't it?" Geoff said, wielding an electric drill.

Then Tom came over to me.

"Elaine put my drawings on the noticeboard in the post office," he explained. "Folk seemed very taken with them, so we had another meeting while you were away and we decided that, if we did as much of the work as we could ourselves, we could stretch the budget."

"Right."

"It just . . . sort of snowballed from there," he continued. "I hope you don't think I was trying to get my ideas through sneakily, while you were away, because honestly it wasn't like that."

"I'm sure it wasn't," I said.

I meant it, too. If he was thinking that, as one of the mainstays of the committee who'd had different ideas from his, I'd feel jealous of his success

Dublin, Ireland.

*Y*OUR *wonderful cover brought back so many memories of a great short break that a friend and I spent in Dublin. We didn't have much money and could only afford to go for four days, but there was so much to do that the time flew by and it was one of the best holidays I have ever had.*

We especially loved the Dublin Flea Market and the live music and excellent food made it a day to remember. My friend bought a second-hand jacket that she wears to this day and still can't believe that it only cost £7!

The pubs and restaurants are fantastic and, by asking around, we managed to find some really reasonable places to eat. We'd both love to go back again and have decided that we're going to save something every month for a year or two and put it aside for a really indulgent break.

I can't wait!

— *Ms J.K., Carlisle.*

J. CAMPBELL KERR.

in my absence, he was wrong. I didn't, not one bit.

I did feel something, though. Some unease, some reservation . . .

Probably because of my awkwardness, it flashed through my mind to ask about receipts for purchases, and insurance arrangements — but such technicalities didn't seem appropriate with all the eager faces around me.

"Give me a few minutes to go home and get changed into my work clothes," I said instead.

Buttercup Days

THE meadow is bright with the beauty of buttercups,
See how they gleam in the sun's golden rays.
Summer's arrived and the countryside's blooming,
How we delight in these buttercup days.

Foxgloves stand tall in the glades in the greenwood,
The delicate dog rose its beauty displays,
Honeybees hover amid the pink clover
Gathering nectar on buttercup days.

In pasture and paddock in June's verdant landscape,
Horses and cattle contentedly gaze,
Now winter is past and living is easy,
They're making the most of these buttercup days.

— *Rosemary Bennett.*

WE worked every weekend through into the summer. Occasionally we needed to hire equipment, or get an expert in. But among us we had representatives from most trades and it was amazing, and inspiring, what we were able to do just using our own combined skills.

I joined the pond-clearing group because it seemed the best way to assure Tom that I didn't hold any grudge.

"It's hard work," he said when I offered, "and messy."

"I'm OK with that," I insisted. "I did most of the work in my cottage myself. It was a wreck when I moved in."

He considered what I'd said in that thoughtful way he had.

"That's different, though, Rose. You were creating your home — working towards a dream of your own."

Like that earlier time we'd spoken, his eyes seemed to challenge me.

And just like before, I remained silent.

Tom was wrong, though. I wasn't working towards my dream — I was trying to forget it . . .

We'd looked at loads of houses, David and I, after we'd become engaged. But, always, he'd found something wrong with them and we'd never got beyond the first viewing.

Then we saw Rose Cottage, here in the tranquillity of the village, but still just twelve miles from the town I'd grown up in and where my family still lived.

I just adored it. And the fact that it shared my name — well, that was a sign, I was sure, that we should go for it.

So instead of accepting David's grumbles about it, like I had with all the others, I dug in. Sure, it needed things done, but we could do them gradually. It was perfectly habitable.

Well, when I dug in, David clambered out. He'd been thinking, he said, and

122

he wasn't ready to get married. That was why he'd found something wrong with every potential home we'd looked at — to put off the day.

I was devastated. All my cherished hopes and plans for our life together — all my dreams — scattered like blossom in the wind, burst like a balloon under a bulldozer.

My attachment to the cottage stayed, though, and I decided to go ahead with it on my own. It was only small, and as I've said, in a bad state of repair. I could afford it — just about.

Even so, it was out of economic necessity that I started doing jobs round the place myself. I realised quite quickly that it was good for me. It kept me from constantly playing in my mind how things might have been. When I'd got it as I wanted, my family said, "Now you can sit in your garden and relax and dream."

Instead I'd kept busy in other ways — like through my involvement with the village hall. The truth was, I didn't "do" dreams any more.

THERE was a weed that grew in the pond, and honestly, however much of it we cut down, twice as much seemed to replace it.

"Like the Hydra." Tom smiled at me when I mentioned it to him.

"Sorry?"

"It's a creature from the Greek legends. You cut off one of its many heads, and it grows more."

We were standing at the water's edge as we spoke, just preparing to wade back in there and tackle some more of the wretched weed, when I lost my footing.

"You all right?" His arm was round me, saving me from falling, quick as a flash.

"Yes, fine," I insisted.

Actually, in truth, I was finding the whole thing a strain. I didn't think it was simply because it was hard and messy work, as Tom had said it would be. OK, I'd been a bit younger when I'd worked on my cottage, but even so, I really didn't think it was that. The strain was more a feeling of general unease. I wished it would hurry up and be done.

Luckily, just a couple of weekends later, we suddenly started seeing the fruits of our labour.

The big windows had now been fitted in the hall, there was an improved kitchen that had been done largely to my original idea *and* my recommended boiler was in there, too! And yet, oddly, it was the pond that was now satisfying me most. Or maybe "fascinating" is a better word . . .

On the Saturday when the kitchen was finally completed, while everyone crowded in, I stayed outside, alone, gazing into the water that was now as clear as glass, sure that it had something to tell me . . . But all I saw was the mosaic of pebbles at the bottom.

LATER, when I was back home, I couldn't settle. So, just as it was starting to get dark, I went for a walk. The pond still beckoned, and I soon ended up back outside the hall. Work was long over for the day, but the smell of timber, varnish and paint lingered and mixed with the flower-scents from the shrubs that had managed to avoid damage during all the upheaval. Soon, new plants would be introduced for the pond —

I jumped as a hand touched my shoulder.

"Tom! You keep doing this, nearly scaring the life out of —"

I broke off as he raised the fingers of one hand to his lips, in a "Sssh!" gesture. With the other hand he gestured in the pond's direction.

I saw it, a heron, standing there on its long graceful legs.

"It's just like in your drawings," I whispered. "Your dream really has come to life."

And then I understood it — the sense of unease I'd been feeling. It was more than unease, actually — it was fear. The fear of ever having another dream, just to watch it break again.

But dreams could come true. Tom's scheme for the hall — which had seemed to be so extravagant, so wild, so impossible — was proof.

All at once, I felt indescribably happy. Trying to get a better look at the heron, I moved carefully forward, quietly, quietly — and tripped!

Once more, Tom's arm shot out and grabbed me.

But this time I didn't pull away, I stayed with his arm round my waist because I wasn't scared any more.

"There is another dream I have," he said eventually, having made no attempt himself to remove his arm. "Will you have a drink with me?" He pointed to the village pub, the Red Lion, just at the other side of the road.

"If you think they'll let us in with our wellies on." I smiled, for we were both still dressed in our work clothes.

As we set off towards the pub, Tom was saying that we could offer to leave our boots at the door, but I didn't think us in our stocking-feet would be any more of an attractive proposition to them. Suddenly there was a swoosh in the growing darkness as the heron soared up into the sky and was away.

I knew it would be back, though. It had found somewhere that it was good to be — and I shared the feeling! ∎

124

Born Free

I HAD already been in Spain for two months and at the estate for a few weeks when I met Allie. She immediately struck me as a girl who'd fit in — lively and enthusiastic. She was pretty, too, with shiny dark brown hair and hazel eyes. Not that I noticed what she looked like (much) when she arrived; I was definitely not on the look-out for a girlfriend that summer.

She was willing to work hard, which I appreciated. I'd come across others — students, people on gap years and so forth — who seemed to think they could come to Spain, muck about in the sunshine, go nice and brown and get paid well for the privilege.

I respect the people here too much for that. If they're kind enough to take me on when my Spanish isn't up to much, then I work hard in exchange. But it's such a great life down here in Andalucia that I don't mind the work. The sleepy villages, the mountainsides cut into terraces with lemon trees that smell so fragrant, and the sunshine. It's unforgettable.

I felt I could be a bit of a guide for Allie. I'd been out here longer, and I had the tan and the back muscles to prove it.

"I'll show you the ropes," I said that evening when she turned up from Malaga in Consuela's old car. "Don't you worry."

by Alison Carter.

Illustration by David McAllister.

She smiled at me, not quite in the way I expected.

"Thanks, Jon," she said. "I bow to your superior knowledge."

"I didn't mean . . ." I muttered, and didn't know what to say next. She had this effect on me (which was quite annoying, as time went on) of making me feel really young when actually I'm twenty-two — twenty-three in November.

The estate at Orviega isn't your usual sort of "working abroad" place. Loads of young people spend time getting some new experiences in other countries, earning a bit to fund their travels and learning a language, but often they go to the cities or the industrial fruit-picking places. I'd opted for something a bit different. It's the way I am. The estate's special. A genuine Andalucian working estate.

"I plan to move around," Allie said. We were collecting eggs from the dusty bantams that scratch around in the coop up behind the manor house. "I've got until Christmas, really, or until the money runs out and I can't find a job. I'm just passing through, to be honest."

"Oh, me, too," I said. "And I chose this place to avoid all that stupid bar work everyone does."

"Too right," she agreed. "Who wants to stand behind a counter on the Costa del Sol while English people order English beer and steak pie?"

I laughed.

"My dad got me this job through a contact," I said. "We have a farm in the Midlands, and there's a kind of information exchange thing going on. He got talking to Señor Ramirez at a conference, and here I am. It's pretty funny: the extreme contrast between the smelly milking units back home and the beauty of this place."

We both straightened up, holding our egg baskets, and looked out across the valley.

THE nearest village looked as though it had been scattered by a careless hand on to the opposite side of the ravine, its buildings pure white in the sunshine. The smell of ripening olives and wild flowers was everywhere. In the far distance, hazy in the hot air, I could see the higher peaks of the Alpujarras range. I breathed in slowly.

"It's a million miles away," Allie said. She shooed the little dark hens gathering round her sandaled feet.

"So, how did you come to join our band of labourers?" I asked.

"Family contacts, too," she said, and blushed slightly. "I have this aunt who has a place on the coast, about an hour away. A second home. She comes up here to eat the organic food, and look at the view. She gets to escape the tourists, she says. So she knows the Ramirez family, and, um . . ."

"Oh, right." I nodded. "Those kind of contacts."

"Jon. I'm no different from you," she said. "I'm willing to work so I can travel and see Spain. I have a nursing course to go to next year, so I want to make the most of the time I have. I'm here for three weeks, then I'm off to Granada. I hope to get a job as a tour guide. My dad —" She stopped.

"Don't tell me, your dad knows the man who owns the Alhambra Palace and he'll give you a job showing people round in English."

She ignored me.

"How long are you staying?"

I shrugged.

"Me, I like to go where the wind blows. I might well head up to the centre. I hear Salamanca's a gem. If I get there when the season's still in full swing then there's sure to be work. I just know that I'm not going to get tied down."

"Tied down?"

"Oh, you know. I was in Madrid for a few weeks — my first stop in the country. Met this guy who was going into a banking job when he got home. Said he wanted to be free and footloose, see the world, be open to anything. He ended up stuck like glue to this girl from Eastbourne or somewhere, practically engaged. Talk about limitation."

Allie screwed up her face. It suited her, with her small nose.

"Ugh," she said. "No way. That's not what I'm looking for. Quite the opposite."

ALLIE fitted in pretty well in the team. There was Dan, a language student on a year out — he had another week or so before he was moving on to the south of France. He already had a job to go to there, harvesting lavender or something.

Georgie was here for the whole summer and into the autumn. She's half Spanish anyway — her mum is from round here and they're always in the Alpujarras. She's putting away money for an archaeology course. I felt that Georgie was an example to me; she was definitely a free spirit, full of stories about her travels and her experiences.

The estate's a sort of farm-cum-hotel-cum-retreat centre, an old house which still has all its original features. There are the weird slate ceilings that you think might fall on you at any moment, but which have stayed put, keeping the place warm in winter and cool in summer, since about the sixteenth century. The floors are black stone, polished by centuries of feet, and there are pots of flowers all over the place — red ones. I can't remember the name, but my mum would tell you. Something beginning with "G".

In the morning it smells of the gorgeous organic bread they bake here, and then later it's the coffee fumes and roasting peppers. In the evening Georgie lays out dishes of figs (they grow them here) or slices of their goats' cheese

— I've learned to milk a goat! So there are always different scents about the place, and all of them gorgeous.

People come here for a break, to walk in the mountains, to eat the home-grown food. The owner, Señor Ramirez, and his family go north in the summer, and that's why they get in help.

So, Allie and I got along fine. We had stuff in common, despite the fact that her family is clearly loaded, and I'm the son of a dairy farmer who's battled BSE, foot-and-mouth and TB, and is never sure where the next bit of cash is coming from. Mainly we both guard our independence.

"Neither of my parents took any time off," she said one night.

We were sitting with Georgie on the big terrace, tired. It was after midnight and the cicadas were chirping away like crazy. Apart from that it was really peaceful. The manor's about half a mile from a road. The quiet is amazing.

"My mum said she's always regretted it," Allie continued. "She really likes my dad, don't get me wrong, but she wishes she'd had a bit of freedom. Got married at twenty-three. She'd never been abroad!"

"I will never marry," Georgie said, putting her feet on the wall. They were tattooed with delicate traceries — she had had that done in India. "I just know it wouldn't suit me."

We both looked at her. Georgie's quite a mature woman — at least thirty-four, I'd say. She knows what she's talking about.

"Yeah, I can go along with that," I said.

Georgie smiled at me. How is it that women always seem to smile at me in a way that's not quite what I expect?

"We'll see, Jon," she said.

Allie sat back with her arms behind her head.

"Nobody's going to tie me down," she said. "Not for years and years."

"You tell 'em," I said.

SEÑOR RAMIREZ had left instructions with the estate manager about our work, and she gave us a task list each day. Consuela also told us to drink plenty of water and to take a proper siesta. I felt I was sort of becoming Spanish, if that makes any sense.

We had the ongoing task of preparing a kitchen garden for planting in the early spring. It was beyond the main farm buildings, a patch dug ages ago out of the slope, but it had been abandoned. Consuela said that olive production had taken over from self-sufficiency as the estate's main source of revenue a hundred years ago or so.

Ten years ago the family had decided to resurrect the farm and turn to organic production. They wanted to make the place a haven for rest and for real food. They run all sorts of courses here: painting, meditation, that kind of

128

Children's Classics

Enid Blyton

ONE of the best-remembered and popular authors of children's literature, Enid Mary Blyton was also possibly the most prolific author of the twentieth century. From the start of her writing career in 1922 until her death, aged seventy-one, in 1968, many hundreds of titles were produced for children of different ages. To date, it is thought her combined book sales total more than 600 million. Sales of the "Famous Five" series still amount to more than one million every year.

Her output was so great, in fact, that some have suspected a ghost-writer must have assisted, though no-one has ever come forward. She also published several titles under the pen-name Mary Pollock, between 1940 and 1943, which was a combination of her middle name and her first married name — she was married twice, first to Hugh Alexander Pollock from 1924 till 1942, and then to Kenneth Waters from 1943 until his death a year before his wife, in 1967.

Although some have accused Blyton's books of being dated and politically incorrect, they continue to win over new audiences today as well as remaining popular with adults. In the BBC's Big Read project to find the nation's favourite book, "The Magic Faraway Tree" series was voted in at number sixty-six, and in 2008, Blyton was voted best-loved author in the Costa Book Awards. Her stories have been translated into ninety languages and are sold worldwide, and she is deemed to be one of the best and most successful children's storytellers of at least the last century, if not of all time. ∎

thing. We don't get involved in those, though. Allie and Dan and I had to weed this vegetable patch — no chemicals allowed here — and improve the soil. It was backbreaking.

"My girlfriend is going to be well impressed with my triceps," Dan announced. He held up a bare arm, pale above the line of the T-shirt he wasn't wearing, and nut-brown lower down.

"Yeah, very nice," Allie said. "Seen enough, thanks. When will you meet up with her?"

Dan sat heavily on the dry earth and gazed longingly up at the cloudless sky.

"Five days and about six hours," he answered. "At the station in Marseilles. She's flying out to meet me there." He sighed.

Allie leaned on her hoe and looked sideways at me. I grinned back. Poor old Dan.

"See," Allie said later as we followed Dan back to the house. "He's practically chained to this girl."

"I know. I spoke to Dan about coming down to Jerez with me when the weather cools, maybe crossing into Portugal in October. But he has to be with the girlfriend."

"It's a common problem," Allie said. "Me, I'm out of here in just less than three weeks. Granada for certain, and then, well, wherever the current takes me."

"I've had a call from this guy I met in Madrid, actually," I said. "Not the one with the girlfriend, another one. He might be lining up a job in a stable, up near Salamanca. That's between Madrid and Portugal."

"I know where it is, thanks," she said.

"Sorry. Anyway, I talked up my experience with horses. I'm telling myself they're no different from cows, once you get to know them."

Allie eyed me doubtfully, in a way that made me laugh. I decided that she was definitely OK.

THE trouble was that, as the weeks passed and I spent time with Allie, the prospect of separating in a few weeks — possibly for ever — became less and less attractive. It was funny how my strongly held beliefs about independence, freedom and all that seemed . . . well . . . weaker.

An annoying image of my mum and dad kept coming to me. I've got a photo of them on my bedroom wall. Well, it's obviously not my bedroom any more — I'm a grown man. I just visit. It's of them on their honeymoon in Southport. That picture always looked comical to me — Mum's funny hairstyle and Dad in a jacket that looks too small. They are smiling so hard, but heading, I know, for domestic life and the farm, and not much in the way of fun.

But I kept thinking, as I laid the sheets out so we could shake the ripe almonds from the trees, or as I swept the patios, of how they're smiling away in that photo. And how they still smile, even when the farm's in trouble. When I'm home, I hear them laughing at practically nothing. I'd never really realised it before.

But Allie wasn't like my mum. No way. She was your classic unchained type. She even said that she was doing that nursing training so she could go to Africa, help out there maybe, see more of the world once she had the skills. Or Asia. She had it all mapped out. At least she had not being mapped out all mapped out, if you see what I mean.

✳   ✳   ✳   ✳

"I like this place so much," she said.

It was early morning. We'd been helping in the kitchen for a change, peeling potatoes (how glamorous!) and we took some of the chef's fabulous coffee out to the garden for a break. It was cool, before the sun began to blaze. A lizard slid into a crack in the pale stone wall. I could see that the bougainvillea would be flowering fully very soon. It promised to be a vibrant purple.

"I almost wish I was staying longer." She looked suddenly at me. "Except I wouldn't," she said quickly. "There's so much still to do, to see."

"Too right," I said. "Go with the flow."

I had to work with Allie nearly every day. She was friendly and chatty. And she was beautiful, so much so that it became difficult to be with her all the time and not say something. It was almost a relief when Consuela asked me to drive to the coast for supplies, or to spend my working day at the top of the estate, clearing the derelict sheds up there.

But I needed to see Allie. Her face became part of the magic of that place. Part of me wanted to avoid her and part of me wanted to roam around the manor and the grounds in case she was out there reading a book. Luckily, she had developed a habit of sitting in a deckchair in the shade of a veranda near the restaurant, so I could generally find her there.

I didn't "pass by" all the time — I didn't want to look like an idiot — but she didn't seem to mind me coming over for the odd chat, even though we did so much on the estate in each other's company. Of course she didn't mind. After all, we got on fine. Two free spirits, sharing our common aim of staying free.

But I was not alone often enough with Allie. I knew that it wouldn't be any use, anyway; she wasn't interested in any sort of a relationship, and she certainly wasn't interested in me. But that couldn't stop me. I turned from the coolest Brit in Andalucia to a lovesick fool in a few short weeks.

I proposed a trip to Córdoba. Consuela gave us the day off. It was miles away, but I knew I'd get the whole train journey to be with Allie.

It was a long journey — a long, hot journey — although Spanish trains are good. And we did have hours to talk: about how fancy-free we were, about how many countries we'd see before we were twenty-five, about the downsides of romantic entanglements, mortgages and marriage.

It was mostly Allie talking, actually. I must have seemed a bit morose. She rambled on, and then apologised for talking too much. We fell asleep.

CÓRDOBA, at least, was amazing. There's this mosque, a vast palace full of columns, made of stone striped in red and gold. It was built centuries ago and it's really cool and atmospheric. And then, just as you're wandering through a forest of those narrow pillars, imagining all the Moorish people who once lived here, you come across a cathedral, a Christian cathedral, right in the middle. I'm not kidding.

The Open Road

A LONG road and an open road,
It's calling me away.
It travels on to distant heights
And beckons me each day.
It passes meadows green and still,
And leaves the town behind,
It shows me sweet serenity
And quiet peace of mind.

"This is . . ." Allie stood looking up at the choir screen, the carvings, the space above our heads where there had been rounded Moorish arches and shady nooks. She'd run out of words.

"I know." I didn't have much to say, either. I think we both saw all the meaning in the two religions, merged like this. It was mind-blowing.

We didn't need to say much. I already knew that Allie and I thought the same about lots of things. We wandered around the city, sat in a café and ate the local pastries and read the guidebook. It would have been a brilliant day if I hadn't known that Harry, now in Salamanca, had arranged that job for me,

J. Winkley.

*It shows me freedom and escape
As problems all take flight,
I feel at one with earth and sky
And find a new delight.
A long road and an open road
With sunshine every day,
And I can travel when I wish —
It's just a thought away!*

— Iris Hesselden.

and that Allie had re~~~~
from the bloke in Grana~~~~

Allie seemed ill at ease on~~~~ trip, too, like she was always abo~~~~ to say something and then decided not to. I wondered if, despite trying not to, I was being a bit obvious.

* * * *

It was a couple of days after the Córdoba trip when I went a bit crazy. Suddenly, the answer seemed so clear. I called Harry and said I was really sorry and could I put off meeting up with him in the Salamanca region, and thanks for the job thing, but I had to cancel.

I didn't tell him why. What sort of a chump would I look like, chasing a girl who wouldn't look at me twice to a large city where I had no job to go to, only about three hundred Euros in my wallet, and where I'd have to do some pretty creative work to be able to "bump into" her? I borrowed a book on the Alhambra from the manor's little library, and wandered round to that veranda which Allie seemed to like so much, although it was a bit too near the bins for my liking.

"Oh, hi," I said lightly, feigning nonchalance.

"Hi." She looked distracted. Her book was upside-down, which was odd. She'd also been reading the same book the whole time she'd been there.

"Listen, have you seen all this stuff about the Alhambra?" I said earnestly. "D'you know there are actual rivers running through it, channelled by the Moorish rulers to cool the palace? And the gardens sound just amazing." I flicked the pages of the book. "I'm actually wondering whether I ought to go there next, just so's I can see it in high summer, get the full benefit."

"It's very busy in August," she said. "Tourists everywhere. You should stick

133

to Salamanca."

There was a short silence.

"Well." I laughed, a stupid, high-pitched laugh. "It's too la —"

"It's funny, you saying that," Allie said, sitting up, interrupting me. "I was thinking that maybe I've had enough sun. I had my 'Lonely Planet' guide out again and that region looks pretty good."

"What region?"

"Castilla-Léon. The university in Salamanca and the bridge on the river are supposed to be lovely — very ancient. I might check that out. You know me, plenty of contacts I can call on. I bet my dad will know someone who knows someone."

"And miss out on Granada, on an actual, probable job? Are you crazy?" I think I almost shouted. My head was beginning to swim. What was she doing changing her plans when I'd bought a ticket to Granada to be near her?

Allie must have been shocked by my tone of voice. She looked crestfallen.

"Sorry. I've been really foolish. I rang home and everything, to tell them I wasn't doing Granada. I somehow thought that . . ." Her voice trailed off. She got up suddenly and dropped her book.

"Wait —" I said, picking it up and following her. I put a hand on her shoulder. It was now or never.

"I bought a ticket for Granada," I began, and I swallowed hard. "You know what I said about being a free spirit? Well I'm not as free as I thought, thanks to you, Allie. I thought that if I followed you to Granada, then . . ." My hand dropped to my side. "I don't know what I thought."

SHE looked at me with those hazel eyes. In that evening light, my goodness, they were beautiful.

"Can I get this straight, Jon," she said quietly. "I changed my plans to follow you to Salamanca, and you changed yours to follow me to Granada?"

I stared at her. In my embarrassment it hadn't occurred to me for a moment that her ideas were anything like mine. She'd said something about less sun, about a university, or a river or something.

It was then that she smiled at me in a certain way, not like all the other smiles she'd sent my way — in a way that was just right, for a change. I was pretty close to her, what with picking up her book and everything, so I kissed her, and the image of that place, and that time, was stamped for ever on my mind. The sweetest moment of my life so far. I wished that someone would take a picture that I could hang on my wall for my children to look at.

"I suppose this means we're going to Granada," she said, "once I can get a ticket. Once I can drag myself away from here."

"I suppose it does," I said, smiling. "We can be free spirits, but together." ■

A Patchwork Of Memories

by Jennifer Young.

Illustration by
Stephanie Axtell.

STEVE looked across the room at the dark-blonde
head bent over a bundle of material. He glanced at the clock, saw its
hands nudging eight.

"Lizzie, I thought you were doing your homework."

"This *is* my homework."

"It doesn't look much like homework to me."

"We had to make something and bring it in. So I thought I'd make a blanket

135

for Freddy."

Lizzie shook the piece of cloth out and looked at it with satisfaction. "What do you think?"

Steve shook his head as he looked fondly at his daughter. Perhaps Jolene had looked like this when she was a ten-year-old? Somewhere, in the boxes and cupboards full of things she'd left behind (the things which he hadn't yet been able to bring himself to sort through after she had passed away), there must be pictures of her at that age.

One day, soon, he'd have to have a look.

"A blanket for a teddy bear? I don't know."

"You have to check it, Miss Forbes said."

"I don't think I know how."

Steve took the square of blue material and turned it over in his hands. The edges were turned over neatly enough, but the stitches were big and uneven, the ends of thread trailing.

"I wanted to do a piece of patchwork." Lizzie reclaimed her work and looked at it critically. "It's quite untidy, isn't it? I was trying to make all the stitches the same size and in a neat line, but they aren't."

"Well, you can tell Miss Forbes I think it's great."

She giggled, then she folded the material, put it neatly into a plastic bag and tucked it into her school backpack.

"Can you teach me to do patchwork, Dad?"

"No. I can't even sew on a button. Come on, Lizzie. Get everything ready for tomorrow and I'll make you some hot chocolate. At least I can do that much around the house."

FROM the kitchen he heard her singing as she packed everything up and he boiled the kettle and put the cocoa in the cup. It was their evening routine, and he treasured it. In the months since Jolene had died he'd come to prize this evening time he spent with his daughter.

Lizzie was so like Jolene, very neat and organised. She liked to make things, to have work in her hands and take pride in it. Recently she'd thrown herself into these things, as if she could somehow hold more closely to her mother's memory by doing all those things that her mother would have taught her, though he could not.

"Come on, then," he said, picking up the mug and carrying it through to the living-room. "Shall we read?"

Usually he read aloud to Lizzie from the stack of old classics which Jolene had kept from her own childhood. She loved to curl up next to him on the sofa and look over his shoulder, even when there were no pictures.

Tonight she shook her head, took her cocoa and sat next to him as usual.

"Did you really like Freddy's cover?"

"Not as much as Freddy will, I'm sure."

"I wanted to make it patchwork. When I was little I had a patchwork blanket for my cot, remember? Mum made it."

"I remember."

Jolene had started stitching it as soon as she knew she was pregnant, sewing through the long summer evenings. The colours had been so bright. Steve remembered the first time they'd tucked Lizzie up under it, on the day they'd brought their new baby home. Presumably it, too, was among those piles of things that Jolene had left, packed up to be cherished and now hidden in a box in the attic.

"I'd like to learn patchwork, Dad. Will you teach me?" Lizzie looked up at him, appealing.

A lump rose in his throat.

"Sweetheart, I told you, I can't sew. Not even a button. I have to get your gran to do the mending!"

"That's terrible," his daughter said gravely. "A grown man who can't sew." Then she twinkled a little smile at him and laughed.

A FEW days later, when Lizzie had gone to bed, Steve sat down with the newspaper and listened to her CD player, playing some soft music as she drifted off to sleep. Now that Jolene was gone — had been gone for six months — Lizzie was his everything.

She sometimes cried for her mother in secret (or so she thought, though he heard her from the next room), denying it when he asked her lest he become upset. But he knew. He knew. After all, he, too, cried sometimes, alone at night.

He waited until the CD had finished playing and the house had lapsed into silence, then went upstairs. Lizzie was almost asleep. Freddy Teddy, tatty but irreplaceable, lay beside her on the pillow, tucked under his coverlet.

"Goodnight, sweetheart."

"Goodnight, Dad."

"Love you."

"Love you, too." A sleepy pause. "Dad?"

"Mm?"

"Remember about the patchwork?"

"Of course."

"I want to make a quilt, like Mum did. I want to be just like Mum."

Steve reached down a hand and stroked her cheek.

"Well, if that's what you want, you can make one."

"Is that a promise? Can I really make one?"

"It's a promise." He turned away.

He lay awake for a long time, knowing he'd made a promise he couldn't keep. He couldn't sew.

Jolene's sewing-machine was hidden away in the cupboard under the stairs; that bit was easy. But he didn't know how to operate it. Plus there was the fact that the memories were still too raw — of Jolene sitting with her sewing spread across her lap, laughing at his incompetence while little Lizzie played with the thread and the shiny buttons Jolene kept in her granny's old tea caddy.

Still, if Lizzie wanted to be like Jolene then he'd help her, no matter what it cost him. Somehow he'd keep his promise to Jolene's daughter.

T HE sewing-machine was more difficult to get at than he'd thought. It had only been six months since Jolene had died, but somehow it had been shoved to the back of the cupboard behind all the sports gear he no longer used, old pictures and piles of recycling.

"Have you got it?" Lizzie was jumping up and down with excitement.

"Not yet, but I can see it. Hold on . . ."

He burrowed into the cupboard again and grasped the handle, hauling it out. It was heavier than he thought.

"Oh, let me see!"

"Wait a moment." He heaved it through the house and on to the dining-room table.

"Open it!"

Steve undid the clips and opened the case. The sewing-machine sat on the table, just as Jolene had left it, navy-blue thread still on the spool.

"Now that we've found it," he said to Lizzie, who stood enraptured with her hands clasped, "I have to confess I don't know how to work it. Any ideas?"

She tiptoed forward to the table and stretched a hand out to touch it as though it were a sacred relic.

"Why don't we ask Sally?"

"Sally?"

"Yes, don't be silly, Dad. You know Sally. Mum's sewing friend."

"Oh, yes. Of course I know Sally."

His memory was one of the things that continually caught him out these days. When he thought of Sally he thought of Jolene. Sally had been Jolene's best friend, her bridesmaid, and had shared her love of sewing. Together the two of them had made her wedding dress.

"They used to sew together. She made me . . ."

"Yes, yes. I know."

It wasn't that he'd forgotten Sally Moffat, just that he'd removed himself from Jolene's friends. Sally had been one of those who'd rallied round, sitting with Jolene for hours, looking after Lizzie, making meals for the freezer and then graciously fading away from the scene when no longer needed.

*   *   *   *

"I'd be delighted to teach you to sew."

Sally Moffat beamed at Lizzie and passed her a plate of biscuits. The

138

conversation had been polite and formal to start, as both adults tiptoed carefully around a shared loss. Once Steve had put forward Lizzie's request, however, their hostess instantly thawed.

Lizzie, at her most grown up, accepted the biscuit.

"Mum loved sewing with you."

"She looked forward to sewing with you, too. When you were older." Sally's eyes moistened as she smiled at the pretty little girl.

"I want to make patchwork."

"Patchwork's fun. You need to make paper templates and then you tack a piece of cloth around it. Do you know what tacking is?"

"Tacking's big stitches to keep things in place. Miss Forbes told me."

"That's right. Then you take all your patches and sew them together." Sally took a couple of square coasters and laid them side by side as an illustration. "Pass me your coaster."

Lizzie passed hers across obediently. Steve passed the coaster across from under his coffee mug and watched.

"Like that. Then you undo the tacking and take the paper out, get a big piece of fabric to make backing, sew it on and there you are. Finished."

She sat back and looked at Lizzie.

"Are you up for it?"

"A real quilt? A big one?"

"A single size one, perhaps. For your bed."

"All right." Lizzie considered carefully. "Where will we get the material?"

"Oh, don't worry about that." Sally got up and smiled across at Steve. "Just a minute."

He could hear her in the next room, opening a cupboard.

"She's nice, isn't she, Daddy?"

He nodded.

"She is."

"Mummy used to take me to her house in the holidays, before she was ill. They talked and I played in the garden."

Sally came back in, carrying a large cardboard box which she placed on the floor.

"Look at all these."

Lizzie jumped off her seat and tiptoed eagerly over to the box.

"Patches. Oh, wow!"

Sally took a handful out and spread them on the carpet.

"Lots of patches. Your mum and I were going to sit down together and make a quilt. This is our start."

"Will there be enough?"

"Oh, nothing like. We'll have to make a lot more."

Steve looked at Lizzie, turning the rainbow patches over and over, spreading them out on the rug. There were bright colours and dark ones, stripes and flowers. Some of them he recognised; some came from Lizzie's baby dresses, the ones which were too stained to be passed on. Some were from clothes he remembered Jolene wearing, when they were just married. The sea of cloth and colour was so vivid with memory that it hurt.

He looked at Sally and Lizzie kneeling together on the floor and a lump rose in his throat.

Sally sat back and looked up at him. She dashed a tear from her eye and he realised how much she'd cared about Jolene, too, that he wasn't the only one who had lost her.

"Is that OK, Steve? You don't mind?"

"Of course not." How could he mind that someone else would teach Lizzie the skills that were so foreign to him?

"Oh, brilliant!" Lizzie said. "When can we start?"

They worked out a routine. Sally ran her own dressmaking business from home and, two days a week, she finished work early, picked Lizzie up from school and took her home. Once her homework was done, the two settled down to work on the quilt. When Steve came back from work he stopped by, brought cake and made coffee.

"This isn't good enough, Dad," Lizzie observed, as he sat reading the paper while they sewed and chatted. "You'll have to help."

"But I can't . . ."

"You could cut out some patches," Sally suggested, handing him scissors, templates and an old cotton skirt.

So, after that, he sat and cut out squares of cloth while the girls worked on sewing them together. On Saturday afternoons they met at Sally's house, and Sally and Lizzie sat together in the garden while he stayed in the kitchen, preparing supper. Gradually, they progressed.

"You need to do something a bit more useful." Lizzie laughed. She laughed a lot more now, Steve noticed. She concentrated much harder on her schoolwork as well as the quilt. More friends came home to play.

But she never wanted to miss her afternoons with Sally.

"Come on, Dad. Pick up a needle."

"I've told you," he said. "I can't sew."

"Nonsense," Sally said encouragingly. "Anyone can sew. Here, try." She held out a needle and a couple of squares of bright cotton.

"You two make your stitches so neat. I couldn't . . ."

"You can tack the material on to the squares for us. Pull up a chair."

After that, on Saturday afternoons, they all sat together in Sally's bright sewing-room, and phoned out for a take-away when their eyes were tired.

Progress on the quilt slowed. Lizzie became less keen to spend time on it and now on Saturdays they did other things — going out for picnics, or walks, or to the pictures.

After several months the quilt was still not finished. It lay spread out on Sally's dining-room table — a rainbow of lives, Steve's and Lizzie's and Sally's all woven together.

Lizzie had insisted that Steve should sew in some squares. He took a whole evening to sew in a patch from one of Jolene's summer dresses, then from one of Lizzie's. The stitches were a little too large and a little too clumsy, but Lizzie just smiled.

"We'll always be able to tell that those are your patches, Dad!"

A T last it was finished. Sally had taken the day off to sew the backing on to it, so that when they came round to see her on Saturday it was hanging pegged out on her line, all its colours rippling in the sun.

"I thought I'd surprise you. What do you think?"

"It's beautiful."

Of course, it was more than that, but Steve couldn't think how to say what he really meant. It wasn't just all the old clothes, it was afternoons after homework, long evenings, take-away meals, walks in the countryside and talking about Jolene.

"Oh!" Lizzie cried, seeing the quilt. She ran across the garden and buried her face in it.

Steve and Sally saw at the same moment that she was crying.

Steve rushed across the lawn.

"Whatever's the matter?"

"It's finished."

Lizzie let go of the quilt and flung her arms round him.

He went down on his knees on the damp grass and hugged her.

"Aren't you glad?"

"I wanted to do it for Mum, but now it's finished I don't know what to do next."

"Well, we can make more," Steve suggested helplessly.

"Of course we can do more," Sally cut in decisively. "The quilt was only the beginning. There's so much more I can teach you. Tell me, can you cook?"

"No."

"Well, why don't we go inside now and see what we can find to make for supper?"

The three of them walked back towards the house. At the back door Steve turned and looked back at the quilt, which fluttered on the line like a banner bearing a message of comfort and healing. And he knew then that the worst had passed. ■

A Favour For A Friend

FIONN cut the withy-willow for the coracle with deft slashes of his knife, his mind grappling with dimensions and how best to make the craft sit correctly in the water. As everyone knew, this was a boat personal to its user, whose height and weight had to be judiciously taken into account.

"You're the best man for the job, Fionn Thomas," Eira had assured him.

He had come across her quite by chance, herding a small gaggle of geese to Llandysul market, and she had stopped to talk. Her brother had a mind to compete in the July coracle races at Cenarth, she said. Please would Fionn make him a craft fit for the job?

"You won't be out of pocket by it. Dewi says you must ask your price."

Fionn had made a small sound of protest in his throat. He and Dewi Jones had been at school together; they'd climbed trees and tickled for trout in the river, teased the girls mercilessly and got up to mischief, as boys do. There was no way he could accept payment for making his friend so everyday an item as a coracle.

"No payment," he said. "I'll do it as a favour."

Now, hefting the cut willow-wands on to his back, he thought of Eira's pretty face and intelligent eyes. Almost overnight, it seemed, she had changed from a coltish girl to a comely young woman and he shook his head in astonishment, enchanted. If she'd asked him to make twenty boats he'd have done it just for her.

Heading home, his thoughts turned yet again to the construction of the craft. Dewi was shorter than himself but muscled and a good deal heavier, and a racing coracle had to skim lightly over the water. The Teifi on which the race took place was foaming and often turbulent from the mountain rains. He'd need to get the proportions exactly right.

He began that evening, shaving the willow laths on a wooden horse his father had once knocked up for the purpose. Da was gone now, and it was up to Fionn to scrape a living for Mam and himself from the few riverside acres that were now his.

"Fionn?" his mother called, coming out of the house. "What are you doing now?"

Fionn explained what had gone on.

142

"Dewi never was a dab hand at coracle making. His always fell to bits the moment they hit the water. Couldn't very well refuse, could I, Mam? Dewi and I were lads together. He'd have done the same for me."

"Tsk!" Glenys Thomas was typically unsmiling. "You should have accepted something for your efforts. It would have cost Dewi a penny or two if he'd gone to Twm Kettle."

Twm Kettle lived in the next village and had been making coracles for many years.

"We've supplies to buy, grains to get in, and not much money to spare. Why don't you think before you act, Fionn?"

by Pamela Kavanagh.

Illustration by David Axtell.

143

This was an old hobby-horse of Mam's, but Fionn was adamant. A friend was a friend and he was not going back on his word.

"Eira will have spoken to Dewi by now, so let's have no more," he said, quite gently, but with the emphasis of inevitability.

Nor was he going to confide how struck he had been with Eira's new comeliness. *Daro!* It would have taken a braver man than he to bring a girl home to their place. He wondered vaguely if all womenfolk had his mother's capacity for being strong-minded where the running of house and home was concerned, and concluded very probably. Da had been very good at disappearing to talk to his pigs at times, and Fionn well knew the reason why.

But then he thought of the spotless home and the mouth-watering meals Mam could concoct out of next to nothing, and his heart softened. Domineering and often difficult to please she might be, but he loved his mother and oh, how she worked! Tirelessly, in the house, on the fields, wherever she was needed. There was no hand like hers for rearing an orphaned lamb or calf.

GLENYS THOMAS returned to the house, clucking to herself, and Fionn went back to his willow paring. Six laths widthways and nine lengthways was the given requirement for a Teifi craft, which differed in type depending on where a man lived and what sort of water had to be encountered. Two additional diagonals were common to all, as was the lack of nails in the woven framework, to avoid friction and encourage resilience.

This seemingly flimsy construction then had to be secured by turning up the ends of the laths and securing them in a gunwale of woven, unsplit hazel rods. A covering of cowhide, a good tarring, and the coracle was ready for use.

Fionn remembered having stored away a prime bit of ash wood that would carve up splendidly for the paddle.

The weather remained fine and each evening he was able to devote some time to his project. By the end of the week the coracle was finished. Fionn's experienced eye took in the flattish prow, curving to the wider part of the vessel where the seat was positioned. Aft of the planked seat, the boat was gratifyingly semi-circular and bulged pleasingly below the gunwales, making it fully capable of navigating the fast-flowing and often querulous waters of the Teifi.

As he had worked he had thought of Eira, her skirts swishing about her bare ankles as she herded the geese, her long fair hair streaming. She'd been a sight for sore eyes and he longed to see her again. And now the coracle was finished he could hike the two miles or so to the Joneses' place and do exactly that.

The next day, Fionn was quick to tackle the chores and finish off the section of ploughing intended for winter wheat. Taking a cleansing dip in the river, he put on some clean clothes, hoisted the coracle on to his back and set off for the Joneses' farm.

Eira was in the garden, digging up potatoes for the pot.

"Hello," she greeted him, straightening. Her gaze fell on the coracle and she gasped. "Oh, Fionn! That's beautiful. Your coracles always look just right."

Under her praise, two high spots of colour touched Fionn's cheekbones.

"I'd have tried it out myself, but you know how it is," he said. "This is made for a heavier boatman than me. Is Dewi around?"

"He's in the byre. I'll call him, shall I?"

Dewi Jones, stocky and dark, looked at the coracle and grinned.

"Thanks, Fionn. I knew you could be relied upon. Let's launch her, see how she goes."

While Dewi paddled his craft to and fro across the churning river, Fionn and Eira watched from the bank.

"There's clever you are," Eira said in her soft sweet voice of the village. "You're wasted farming that scrap of land, Fionn Thomas. A fortune you'd make, making coracles and selling them."

"Do you think so?"

"I know it. It's said old Twm Kettle is talking about throwing it in, what with his rheumatics getting worse and him feeling the cold more these days. Oh, I know people hereabouts tend to knock up a coracle for themselves, but there's no-one can make them to your standard. You couldn't go wrong, Fionn."

Looking into her eager face, an idea took shape in his mind. If Dewi were to win the race . . . If word spread as to who had made the winning coracle . . . If Mam were there, watching the race alongside the rest of them . . .

"Eira," he said. "Shall we train Dewi up?"

"Well, all right. When shall we start?"

"How about right now?" Fionn replied.

AFTER that, every evening when all the work was done, the three of them took the coracle to a quiet spot where the river ran wide and deep, and Dewi was put through his paces. Honed to fitness by long hours working on the fields, he soon mastered the art of paddling his craft across the water in record time.

Fionn, watching from the riverbank, felt a burst of pride at his handiwork. The little craft fitted his friend so snugly that man and boat seemed almost one entity.

Eira was in charge of the timing.

"Four minutes!" she cried one night as Dewi came paddling up. "No-one can possibly beat that."

"I wouldn't be so sure," Dewi said breathlessly, shaking the droplets of water from his hair. "They're all at it, up and down the river. Practising like the very fury. My Delyth said her brother did the stretch by the bridge in three minutes fifty-five seconds."

Delyth was Dewi's betrothed. The date was set for after the harvest. Would the church bells ring one day for himself and Eira, Fionn thought suddenly with longing. He knew by now that he loved her, but was it returned?

"The river's narrower at that point," Eira said loyally to her brother. "And anyway, his coracle won't be as good as yours."

"All the same, better keep up the good work. Come on, I've got my breath back and it's still daylight. Let's give it another go."

They continued till the first stars appeared overhead and the air flickered with bats' wings. Then, weary but still jovial, Dewi pulled the coracle from the water and hitched it on to his back.

"Better check the herd before I go in," he said. "See you tomorrow, Fionn?"

"I'll be here," Fionn said.

Alone with Eira for the first time, the starlight turning her fair hair to silver, he took her in his arms and kissed her, rejoicing at how surely she yielded to his embrace. She felt like a quivering little bird in his arms. Her lips tasted of wine and all things good.

They broke apart at last.

"Ah, Eira, *cariad*, I love you," Fionn said throatily.

"I love you, too," she whispered, her face a pale blur in the dimness.

"Will you walk out with me?"

"Yes, oh, yes. I'll be proud to." She hesitated, biting her lip. "There's your mam."

It was no secret that Glenys Thomas was possessive where her one and only son was concerned. A good, God-fearing woman, mainstay of the chapel and always ready to do her bit for the village, she was highly respected and held somewhat in awe by many. Providence help the girl Fionn brings home, was the general opinion — always behind closed doors, of course.

Fionn just smiled.

"You leave Mam to me," he said easily.

"You're walking out with Eira Jones?" Glenys Thomas clucked her tongue in disapproval. "The Joneses are Church, you know, not Chapel."

"I know that, Mam. Dewi sings in the choir. Eira can sing as well. Lovely voice she's got — like a lark on a summer morning."

"Tsk! That's as maybe. Doesn't mean you have to get serious about her."

"Mam, a house with music in it can't be bad."

"What a lot of taradiddle! There's more to marriage than singing and music! I knew nothing good would come of making that coracle for Dewi Jones!" Glenys Thomas said with a sniff.

146

Southwold, Suffolk, England.

MY sons used to love their summer holidays in Southwold. We would book into a bed and breakfast and hire a beach hut for a week, but it sometimes seemed to me that we would have been better staying in the beach hut as the children loved it so much. If only those beach huts had had running water and toilets!

When we could drag the boys away from their sandcastles and games, we would visit the lighthouse and the pier. Southwold always seemed like the perfect place for a holiday to me and it was lovely to have my memories of those long-forgotten days brought so vividly to life again.

— Mrs I.J., London.

J. CAMPBELL KERR.

Fionn went for a diplomatic change of topic. He knew Mam probably better than she knew herself. A little patience and tact was all that was needed here.

THE summer slipped by with hot sunshine, gentle breezes and sifting mountain rain. Fionn made his modest leas of hay, milked his few cows, tended his small flock of sheep. The coracle training continued, and somehow in between tending his little farm and helping his friend, Fionn found time to court the girl who had claimed his heart.

The Jones family had a bigger farm and were considerably more outgoing than the Thomases. When the Eisteddfod came to Carmarthen, Eira was there, singing and dancing with the other girls from the village. Fionn had written a poem — in fact, he wrote many and had gathered together quite an anthology, entered in a small leather-bound book which he showed only to Eira. Entranced, she persuaded him to take part in the poetry section. Apart from reading a text in chapel it was the first time Fionn had performed in public, and the thought of sharing his emotions and inner thoughts with such a vast assembly of people was daunting.

As it turned out, he need not have worried. His words on young love and the soft breath of summer stirred the hearts of the audience. There wasn't a dry eye in the house and Fionn, to his utter amazement, was awarded a placing for lyric verse.

Eira threw her arms around him and kissed him soundly.

"Oh, I was so proud! They were all talking about you. I wanted to shout it from the rooftops that it was my man they were going on about!"

Her man. It could not get much better, Fionn thought. All he needed now was to get Mam on their side and things would be perfect. He made a worshipful wish for success at the coracle races.

But before the race, on the very evening before the big day, calamity struck.

✳ ✳ ✳ ✳

Fionn and his mother had just sat down to supper when there was the sound of running feet on the path, followed by an urgent tap on the door.

"Come in," Glenys called.

The door opened to admit Eira. Dishevelled, clearly troubled and out of breath, as if she had run all the way there, she gasped out her story.

"Oh, Fionn. Mrs Thomas — there's sorry I am to interrupt your meal." She made a small gesture of apology with her hand and turned her attention back to Fionn. "Something dreadful has happened. Dewi was getting in some extra practice with the coracle, and like a fool he forgot the paddle and left the boat on the bank while he went to fetch it. While he was gone the cows went down to the water to drink and oh . . . what do you think? The clumsy things have trampled it to matchwood!"

Fionn's heart dropped. It was more than a disappointment for his friend. It was the end of all Fionn's hopes and dreams. Then he rallied.

"I've got some withy-sticks left over. I'll make a new coracle," he said.

"But it's the races tomorrow," his mother cried. "You'll never have it ready in time."

"I'll have a good try."

"Is there anything I can do to help?" Eira said.

"Well, you could sort out the withies for me," Fionn said.

"No-one works well on an empty stomach," his mother put in, unbending a little. "Finish your supper first. I'll put you up a flagon of ale and some sandwiches for later on. It'll help keep you going."

Out in the barn he set to work, stripping the bark, measuring, weaving the selected withy-wands. Dusk fell and Eira, who had done all she could to assist, headed home to tell her brother what was happening.

All night Fionn laboured. As the eastern sky brightened towards dawn he was painting a layer of pitch on the new boat. Normally he would have waited for it to dry and added a second coat, but there was no time for that now. Rubbing his stubbly chin wearily with his hand, he left the craft upside-down in the strengthening sun to dry and took himself off to fetch in the cows for milking. To his surprise his mother was there before him, a steaming mug of strong, sweet tea in her hand.

"I'll see to the cows today," she said, passing him the tea. "You look tired to death. Get this inside you. Then go in and get some breakfast. There's porridge in the pot."

FED, washed and shaved and into clean clothes, Fionn felt much better. The coracle racing was a main event in the area and Glenys Thomas was taking a break from the daily round for once to go and watch.

Fionn harnessed up the pony and trap and he and his mother joined the flow of villagers, farmers and hill shepherds on the road to Cenarth, all bound for the event. Many foot-travellers were taking part and had their coracles strapped to their backs. As they grew closer to the grey-stone village with its dancing river and sparkling falls, Fionn's insides began to churn. So much depended on today. He had never felt so nervous in all his life.

Eira was already there, slender and pretty in a gown of pale blue muslin.

"Fionn! I've been watching out for you. Mrs Thomas — good morning. How are you?"

"Good morning. Well enough, thank you." Glenys Thomas looked into the girl's smiling face and to Fionn's delight her lips, not given to smiling, managed a responsive twitch. His heart warmed to see it. Nobody, not even Mam, it seemed, was immune to Eira's charms.

Dewi arrived, bold and joking, slapping Fionn on the back.

"Fionn, man. All ready for the fun?"

Pretty Delyth Hughes was at his side. Fionn sent her a smiling nod before greeting his friend.

"Morning, Dewi. More to the point, are you ready?"

"Oh, well, you know me, man. Always game for anything. Is that the boat?"

"It is."

Handing the little craft over, Fionn felt a stab of fearful doubt. Every boat was different and none more so than the coracle. Not made to any specific dimensions, the item was very much of the moment. How was he to know that his memory had served him correctly during his long overnight sojourn, and that this new boat was an exact replica of the other? As far as he could tell, it was. Or was it? Dewi would have become used to his craft. Would this one have a different handle and therefore blight his chances?

"You might want to try it out before the races begin," Fionn suggested.

At that moment there was a bellowed call for all competitors to assemble at the riverside. The first of the heats was announced.

"Too late," Dewi replied. "Don't worry. There's nothing like a Fionn Thomas boat. This one's sure to be as good as the last." He delivered Fionn another backslap that all but knocked him breathless. "Wish me luck, then."

Willie Shand.

T O cries of encouragement all round to which his mother, Fionn saw, added her own small word of cheer, Dewi Jones shouldered the coracle and joined the other competitors at the riverside.

On the stone bridge where there was a good view of the proceedings, they all gathered to watch. Faces were excited, breaths held as the first eight competitors, Dewi amongst them, launched and boarded their bobbing coracles. A pause elapsed while the craft were eased into line. On the other side of the bridge the river, flowing directly from the falls, was swift and fierce. But here the water flowed wide and deep and was ideal for the races.

The starting flag was lowered; the race began. People hollered, children squealed, dogs barked — everyone shouted for a favourite. Fionn was aware of

150

Dreams Of Twilight

RIPE fruit tumble off
the bough —
The season has begun.
Burnished conkers clasp
the earth,
Scattered 'neath the
evening sun.

And so, in dreams
of twilight,
Twixt shades red,
amber, gold,
Shedding light in
splendour,
Crisp leaves in
glorious folds.

How lovely is the autumn,
When she twirls her
golden gown,
To strains of
mellow music,
Beauty haunts us
all around.

— *Dorothy McGregor.*

Eira clutching his arm painfully. She knew as well as he what a challenge it was to navigate a boat cold. Would Dewi be able to get to grips with it?

But Dewi Jones was no novice. A few strokes of the paddle and he had the measure of the flimsy little craft his friend had spent the whole night making. He was pulling ahead, bending his back into the work.

"Dewi! Dewi!" the crowd roared, and Fionn, shouting along with the rest, watched, incredulous, as the gap widened between his friend and the competitor in his wake.

"He's there! He's done it!" Eira screeched. "He's won his heat!"

And later, in the finals, Dewi Jones triumphed again!

✳ ✳ ✳ ✳

"All due to you," Dewi said to Fionn, the annual trophy at his elbow.

It was celebrations all round. The ale flowed. Glenys Thomas, it was noticed, allowed herself a sip of something stronger than her usual cup of tea to toast her son's success at making the fastest coracle on the river.

"Wasn't only due to me," Fionn said. "She had the best navigator, too."

Eira slipped her arm in his.

"You'll be surprised when you hear how many people want a Fionn Thomas coracle. Looks like you're in business, Fionn. Ten orders I've taken so far. Ten! I've made sure and told everyone they don't come cheap."

She named a sum that made Glenys Thomas choke on her drink.

"All Eira's idea," Fionn told his mother. "Making coracles could turn out a lucrative sideline, maybe develop into something more. Not daft, is she, Mam?"

"No, indeed," his mother said. She looked at Eira and smiled, a genuine, wide smile that made her look quite different. "Well, now, I never thought I'd ever hear myself say this, but if there's anyone right for my boy it's you, Eira Jones."

Fionn fetched his girl a wink. He'd known his mother would come round in the end. From now on, everything should be plain sailing. ▪

Branching Out

by Pauline Kelly.

PAIGE'S TIMBER

Illustration by
Pat Gregory.

BRASHING," Ryan said, airing his new-found knowledge. "Clearing the woodland and forest of unnecessary growth is called brashing. Not pruning. That's a different thing entirely."

Lori sighed. Ever since her brother had got a place on the forestry course at college he had been unbearable. Yesterday, there had been raised voices between him and Dad. Even Mum was losing patience.

"Brashing, then," Lori said. "Only John and I are thinking of having a solid-fuel burner installed in our lounge and we were wondering whether to go for a multi-fuel or one that burns just wood. I thought wood might be better for the environment and more cost effective, if we could find someone who deals in old stuff — like the clippings after an orchard has been pruned. Or do I mean brashed?"

"You got it first time. Orchard trees are pruned. But you'd need logs, not prunings, for a stove, and it would have to be seasoned stuff, otherwise you'd get a build-up of tar."

"I see. Does anyone deliver to our area, do you think? I've seen a coal lorry. No logs, though. I suppose it is more of a country fuel."

"How should I know?" Ryan said grumpily. "You'd have to make enquiries before you go ahead. There's no point in having a wood-burning stove if you can't get the right stuff for it.

"Look, I've got to be at college for ten. It's time I was off."

Ryan seized the canvas bag containing his woodman's tools and his packed lunch and left, slamming the front door behind him. He made a run for it and just caught the bus as it was about to leave. Showing the driver his student bus pass, he chucked his bag on to the first vacant seat and flopped down beside it.

The journey to college took about half an hour, depending on the traffic. Ryan fixed his gaze on the passing shops and bustling pavements, his mind on Jinnie.

Jinnie Paige was a fellow first-year student — and that was all he knew about her. Try as he might, nothing Ryan did could raise her interest. It had been six weeks now since he had spied her, sitting by the window in readiness for the first lecture of the term, a calm-looking blonde neatly attired in regulation jeans and T-shirt.

"Hi," he had said, parking himself at the desk next to her.

"I'm Ryan Carstairs. And you're Jinnie." He'd already worked that out from the list of names on the noticeboard.

"Correct." She'd sent him a piercing blue glance that was decidedly frosty, before turning her attention to the computer screen on her desk, which for some reason had started to play up.

"You can swap with me, if you like," Ryan had offered. "This one seems to be working OK."

She'd shaken her head, long, golden hair flying.

"It's all right. I'm happier by the window. I don't suppose we'll use the IT facility much today in any case."

She'd turned her gaze pointedly on the view of distant hills, and Ryan had felt firmly put in his place. He'd been a bit miffed. Girls never gave him the cold shoulder. This one could be written off his Christmas card list for sure.

Even as he'd thought it he'd known it wasn't true. She was different from any other girl he'd ever known. No multi-hued hair done up in spikes, no nose stud or little row of earrings . . . not even single ones in gold like his mum wore. All the female embellishments he had previously considered cool were lacking, and somehow they weren't cool any more, either.

Ryan had darted a glance at the soft fall of hair against a smooth cheek that owed nothing to creams or powder, and had known he was smitten.

Very gradually he'd learned, from quiet investigation, something of her background. She was a country girl who travelled in every day in her own car. Bit by bit he'd put together a mental picture. Biggish house in a well-kept garden, privileged upbringing. Private education, probably. Swimming pool, tennis parties — way out of his league.

Then again, if this was the case, what on earth was she doing on a forestry course with a bunch of townies, some of whom were hard put to tell an oak from a sycamore?

It was a mystery that only added to her attraction.

THE bus, which had stopped to pick up more passengers, now set off again, rumbling along the narrow streets of the old town, pausing at traffic lights and pedestrian crossings, weaving between rows of older terraced houses and estates of newer properties, pressing ever onwards on its slow crawl towards the college on the interchange to the new bypass.

There at last, Ryan leaped off the bus and sprinted to catch up with some of his mates who were entering the college gates.

"Hi, Ryan," one of them greeted him. "Field work today and it looks like rain. Hope you've brought a coat. Last time we were in the forest there was a downpour and we all got drenched."

"Tell me about it!" Ryan grinned.

At that moment Jinnie went by in her red car. She didn't acknowledge any of them, but drove carefully past and turned in at the students' parking ground.

"Snooty piece," one of the lads muttered.

"I wouldn't say that," Ryan said. "She was keeping her eye on the road."

"Come on! Jinnie Paige never opens her mouth unless she has to. She thinks she's a cut above the rest of us."

"Maybe she's shy," Ryan said.

He didn't for one moment believe it. Girls like Jinnie had a built-in confidence that was enviable. How he longed to break through that icy Nordic façade and persuade her to go out with him.

He didn't rate his chances. Jinnie had a way of keeping the world at a distance. She answered politely when spoken to, never missed a lecture or practical session, was never late and took herself off promptly when the college day was over, driving away smartly in her little red car.

Day after day Ryan told himself to forget her. The simple fact was, he couldn't.

The minibus that was to take them up-country to the stretch of forest used by the college was waiting outside the main building. The lads put on a spurt and boarded it, making straight for the rear seats where they could all be together.

There were ten on today's venture — seven boys and three girls, including Jinnie. The other two had chummed up and were already seated. Presently Jinnie appeared, taking the empty place closest to them.

Lastly came their lecturer, Jimmy Hough, a bearded and popular character with a cheerful grin.

"Are we all present?" he asked, quickly surveying his group.

"Right then, driver. Let's get rolling."

Coppicing was on the agenda today. October had dressed the woods in flame and bronze and gold, and the hazel coppice was full of squirrels raiding the trees of their fruit for winter larders.

Briefly Jimmy Hough outlined the uses of coppicing and set the group making hurdles. Ryan, inexpertly weaving his hazel rods in and out — nothing was ever as simple as it looked — cast a curious eye on Jinnie's efforts. As on previous practical sessions she was more deft than any of them and had her specimen finished first.

"I think you've done this before," the professor said astutely.

Jinnie nodded.

"I have, actually. More as a hobby."

That was it, Ryan thought. She was using college as a pastime. It was a funny subject for a girl to dabble in, but as his dad often said, there was no accounting for folk.

At midday they broke for lunch. Sandwich boxes were opened and talk centred around forestry and what they all aimed to do once they were qualified.

Ryan, having no idea where his future lay, tended to keep out of these conversations. He knew he enjoyed being out of doors, liked the forests and woodland, and was fascinated by the plant and animal life to be found in them. Sometimes he imagined himself as manager of a country estate, or going abroad to work in the conifer plantations of the northern lands, or maybe heading south to the rainforests.

Ryan knew these to be dreams. More probably he would end up like the professor, lecturing to a bunch of would-be foresters year in, year out, with a mortgage and a family to fend for — which, when he thought about it, wasn't a bad prospect at all.

He came round to one of the group saying his grandfather had been a logger. Ryan was reminded of Lori's words earlier.

"It's not a bad trade to be in, logging. I don't suppose anyone knows of a log delivery service into town?" he enquired hopefully. "My sister's thinking of getting a wood burner. There's a coal man calling at the housing estate where Lori lives. No logs, though."

There was a moment's silence. Then, to Ryan's utter surprise, Jinnie piped up.

"My father runs a firewood business. I'll give you his card to pass on to your sister. I don't have one on me at present. Will tomorrow be all right?"

"Yes. Fine. Thanks," Ryan said, his heart crashing about wildly in his chest.

Jinnie, giving him the faintest of smiles, turned her attention back to the apple she was eating.

Here was the opportunity he had hoped for, Ryan thought. Surreptitiously he put his hand behind his back and touched the smooth bark of the hazel tree he was leaning against. Touching wood was a trait of his mum's. Mum vowed there was nothing to be lost by encouraging fate and everything to be gained. Ryan only hoped that Mum had got it right.

THE next morning Ryan made sure he was wearing his best jeans and the trendy black polo shirt Lori had given him for his birthday. He brushed his wavy brown hair, splashed on some aftershave, and made sure the smile he presented was his most winning.

As it turned out, his efforts were a waste of time. On reaching his desk he found, tucked into the front of the computer screen, the small white business card as promised. Jinnie had come early and was immersed in her current project.

Ryan cleared his throat.

"Um, thanks for this," he proffered.

"No problem." Her eyes never left the screen. "Tell your sister to ring the number. She'll find out all she wants to know."

Ryan glanced at the card in his hand. *T.S. Paige*, it said. *Wood Merchant, Highlea, Hampton Green.* An upmarket address if ever there was one. Most likely her dad owned half-a-dozen such businesses and ran them from home.

Ryan put the card in his pocket to pass on to Lori and headed off for the common room, from where voices and laughter could be heard. He didn't see Jinnie watch him leave the room. Her expression was wistful.

After that Ryan decided not to pursue the Jinnie quest. He flung his energies into his college work, knocked about with the crowd and to all intents and purposes was his usual extrovert self. Only those closest to him saw a change.

"Ryan's quieter," Lori said to her mother. "Do you think he's growing up at last?"

Elcho Castle, Perthshire, Scotland.

I'D be the first to admit that I'm not the greatest lover of ruined castles and ancient history. I find it difficult to imagine people really living in old ruins and can't picture what their day-to-day lives would have been like.

All that changed, however, when I visited Elcho Castle in Perthshire. My husband was playing golf nearby and, finding myself at a loose end, I was delighted when a lady at the hotel asked me if I wanted to accompany her on a day out.

I'd never even heard of Elcho Castle and was amazed to find how well preserved it was. I certainly wouldn't have liked to be a kitchen maid in that kitchen with its huge imposing fireplace and ovens, nor would I have liked to struggle up and down those spiral staircases with piles of bedlinen or hot water for washing!

It was the first time I could really see how people had lived and was a complete step back in time for me. It certainly made me appreciate today's modern conveniences!

— Mrs J.D., Doncaster.

J. CAMPBELL KERR.

Mum was quick to spring to her son's defence.

"He works hard. He's either out on those field studies or up in his room on the computer. You wouldn't believe what a big subject forestry is."

"Oh, it always was an exacting science, Mum. Did I mention we're going ahead with the wood-burner idea? Ryan found us someone who'll deliver at very reasonable rates."

"You'll be nice and cosy," Mum said enviously. "I wouldn't mind having our chimney in here opened up. There's nothing like a proper log fire. I might have a word with your dad."

In due course Lori and John's stove was installed and a load of logs delivered.

"It's perfect," Lori told her brother. "No trouble at all to clean out and we're beautifully warm."

"The log company didn't mind trailing out to you, then?" Ryan asked.

He was still haunted by a pair of bright blue eyes and yellow hair.

"Not a bit," Lori replied. "In fact, we're putting more business their way. Our next-door neighbours like our stove so much that they've decided to go for one as well. Then, yesterday, a woman from across the avenue stopped me to ask about it. It seems we're starting a trend. You could do worse than go into the logging trade once you're qualified, Ryan."

"And set up in competition to Paige's?" He made a wry face. "Some hope!"

CHRISTMAS approached and with it the end-of-term bash. The third-year students on the entertainments committee had engaged a jazz band and were putting on a pretty good festive spread.

Ryan wondered if Jinnie would be there. He tried to picture her all done up for the evening. Anyone who looked so good in jeans and woolly sweaters had to be stunning decked out in her best.

In the next breath he was reproaching himself. Jinnie Paige at a student gig? Get a grip! The moment the final lecture of term is over she'll be bombing off in her little red car, and that'll be the last anyone sees of her till January.

A cold snap sent all the householders turning up their heating. Ryan's mum increased her pressure to have an open fire in the living-room, and this time won her case. Lori rang.

"Ryan? Oh, great. Would you mind doing me a favour?"

"It depends," Ryan said guardedly.

The last favour for his sister involved housesitting while they went on holiday. It had been high summer, with lawns to mow, flower-beds to tend, roses to dead-head. The list had been endless.

"I'll treat you to that DVD you wanted if you'll say yes."

"What do you want me to do?" Ryan said, tempted.

"We thought we'd pop up and see John's parents on Saturday. It's the only one we've got free this side of Christmas. The trouble is I've ordered more logs and that's when they're being delivered. We generally help whoever brings it to unload. Well, I'd rather it was stacked tidily."

At this point Ryan groaned. It was, as he'd thought, never that simple!

"Ryan? Are you still there? You will come, won't you? I'll leave you something to eat and I promise you won't be kept hanging about."

"I'd better not be. It's the college Christmas bash. It starts at eight and I'll need time to get ready."

"They said around one o'clock. That gives you tons of time. Don't forget your key."

Ryan sighed as he replaced the receiver. At least he wasn't expected to dig up the Christmas tree from the bottom of the garden — Lori was one of those clever folk who managed to keep hers going from year to year — and fix the fairy lights. Unloading a few logs was a snip, really.

Lori's place was on the opposite side of town, but that was no problem on his mountain bike. If he was smart he should be back in plenty of time to get ready for the bash.

In the event he was delayed, due to helping Dad remove the boarding from the chimney opening in the living-room, and then taking the now defunct electric fire to old Mrs Mosely three streets away.

Mrs Mosely was delighted to give it a home and showed her appreciation by plying him with tea and mouth-watering home-made mince-pies. By the time Ryan had cycled out to the estate where Lori and John lived, the wood merchant's truck had arrived and the lad was in the process of unloading the bags of logs on to the drive.

"Hi. Sorry I'm late," Ryan called, dismounting and hitching his bike against the house wall.

"Here, let me unlock the garage, then we can put them straight in."

He stopped abruptly. It wasn't a lad at all.

"Jinnie!" Ryan gasped.

She wore a shabby old jacket over her jeans and had bundled her hair up into a peaked cap. The lorry, loaded to the gunnels, foretold a hard afternoon's work ahead.

"Jinnie?" Ryan repeated. "You, on the log round? What's this all about?"

Guilty colour flooded Jinnie's face.

"I might have known I wouldn't get away with things indefinitely. I told you my father was in the logging trade. Well, Dad hasn't been doing it for long. He was in communications before, but he was made redundant and he decided he'd work for himself in future.

"There's always a risk involved when you start up on your own. Making the deliveries when Dad is otherwise occupied is my contribution. Till the business gets on its feet, that is. Mum takes the orders and does the books, so between us things are working out OK. I enjoy the log round. It's hard work but I'm stronger than I look."

"No wonder we never see you at the college socials."

"No time." She smiled ruefully.

"Keeping strictly to work hours seemed the only way I could get my forestry degree and help Dad as well. There's quite a lot involved in a wood business. Lots of red tape, you know."

"I can imagine. Well, I dunno. And I thought it was me. I thought you didn't like me much."

She bit her lip.

"No, that wasn't the case at all. Ryan, I'm sorry to have given you the wrong impression. At first, it seemed the best way of going about things, but then I'd hear you all laughing and joking together and I knew it had been a mistake. I'd earned myself an unfriendly label. I suppose it's too late now to change," she finished in a low voice.

"No way is it!"

A perilous joy was unfolding within Ryan. He drew a deep breath.

"Jinnie, it's the Christmas bash tonight. Would you come with me?" he asked.

She smiled up at him, delight in her eyes.

"I'd love to. The trouble is, the log round. I've still to go back home for another load. Then I'll need to get cleaned up and —"

"I'll help you with the deliveries," Ryan offered.

"We can shove my bike on the wagon. Come on, let's get this lot unloaded."

They stacked the bags of logs into the corner of the double garage and set off for the next port of call. Trade was on the increase, Jinnie said as they rumbled along. More and more people were changing to wood-stoves or open fires.

"I don't know what will happen when the forests run out of ready stock," she finished with a small laugh.

"It shouldn't be a problem. Trees are growing all the time. It won't run out, not if it's properly managed. Forestry's a great career to follow. What d'you want to do once you're qualified?"

"Forest management, like you just said. I quite fancy running summer courses. Dad's business should be established by the time I've got my degree. He wants to diversify and this seems a good route to follow."

"Great. You plan to stick in the area, then? Me, too." Ryan caught Jinnie's

Gingerbread Joe

I'M Gingerbread Joe
And I live on this tree.
And though it may prickle
I'm sure you'll agree
No home could be nicer,
It twinkles with light,
With views of the hearthside,
So cheerful and bright.
For later, I've heard,
Father Christmas will call,
He'll pop down the chimney
With presents for all.
I'll give him a wave,
And I hope that he'll see
I'm Gingerbread Joe
And I live on this tree!

— **Maggie Ingall.**

160

eye, and felt his heart flip when she gave him the full force of her smile.

Between the two of them they quickly had all the orders delivered. Soon they were driving out of the town and through straggling suburbs to the open country beyond, where Jinnie pulled into the driveway of a smallish house, not a mansion at all, in a pretty garden.

There was a spacious yard, beyond which a vast polytunnel had been erected for storing the wood. A small tractor and trailer was parked nearby.

"Good," Jinnie said, jumping down from the cabin.

"Dad's home. He can help us load up. Oh, here he is. And Mum. Mum, Dad, this is Ryan. He's helping me with the round today and then we're going to the college dance."

"Wonderful!" Mrs Paige, a more mature version of her daughter, couldn't have looked more pleased.

Both parents greeted Ryan warmly and he was invited in for a cup of coffee. Time, however, was at a premium. The invitation was kept open for another day and all hands were put towards the reloading of the lorry.

Presently they were chugging out of the yard and on their way again, and as the short December day thickened to dusk they were making their final call. Ryan unshipped his cycle, and arrangements were made for the evening ahead.

"I'll meet you at the college," Jinnie said, her face glowing.

"I can't wait."

He placed his hands gently on her shoulders and pressed a kiss on her lips. She tasted of honey and all things good. She'd be the loveliest girl there tonight, and she was all his. Ryan couldn't think of a better start to Christmas.

"I KNEW there had to be a girl in it somewhere," Lori said, toasting herself in front of a fragrant cherry-wood fire.

"What I didn't know was that she's the girl who brings our logs!"

"It's a small world, isn't it?" Mum replied comfortably.

"Imagine — if John and I hadn't gone eco-friendly, this might never have happened."

"It just shows there's more to touching wood than folk give credit for!" her mother finished happily. ■

Holding On To Happiness

by Melissa Banks.

I T just feels odd," Sian said. "The house is so quiet."

"It suits me fine." Neil laughed. "Much as I love the children, an afternoon off is exactly what we need." He looked at the clock.

"Your sister will walk through that door in five-and-a-half hours and I plan to make the most of every minute until then, starting with this." He kissed his wife slowly.

"Now, when do we have time for something as nice as that?"

They had the chance to talk and to enjoy each other's company that day. It was growing dark when Sian went to close the living-room curtains.

"It'll be a cold night again," she said. "Oh, that's Tansy's leaf." There was a note of unease in her voice.

"Leaf?" Neil joined her at the window. On the pale paving below the window, a black skeleton lay, a perfect pattern of the leaf's structure visible against the stone.

Sian nodded.

"From her ice store."

"You've lost me," he said.

"Oh, you know how Tansy is, collecting things. Yesterday morning we went for a walk, and she found a clean, pure sheet of ice over a puddle. In it, flat as anything, beautifully preserved, was that leaf.

"And didn't you hear her getting worked up about it today, before Betty picked them up? She was angry that the ice was beginning to melt. The corner of the leaf was showing."

"She's a funny little thing. Don't they say that the third child is the eccentric?"

"She's like me." Sian smiled.

"That's true," he agreed. "Doesn't respond well to change."

162

Later, Neil found Sian looking at the leaf at the kitchen table.

"The ice store again?" he asked.

"Not ice now," Sian replied. "It's just going to rot."

"And no doubt Tansy will cherish it until she forgets, and we find it stuck to a piece of furniture." He sat down opposite her.

"Can I get you a lovely, frothy cup of coffee? Sian? What is it?"

"Nothing at all," she said, wiping away a tear.

"Darling."

"It's . . . this makes me think how . . . how short-lived everything is."

"It depends on how you look at it."

"I'm such an idiot." She shook her head. "It's just that sometimes, when I look at how good everything is — you, the children, our life — it makes me anxious about how long it will last."

He nodded, understanding now.

"Sian, it will last. We had a tough time once, and it's made you think every good thing can be . . . damaged."

"Well, it can."

"And it can mend."

There was no need for either

The Nativity

A **SOLEMN** *little shepherd,*
Dressed up in robes of beige,
Meekly walks along the hall
To find his place on stage.

A woolly sheep is dragged along
By another little boy;
Its ears hang down, its wool's so thin —
It's such a well-loved toy!

And centre stage young Mary sits,
She so wants to impress.
She nervously anticipates
And fiddles with her dress.

The teacher, so professional,
With baton held aloft,
The silence almost filled the room
Until somebody coughed!

of them to say what was in their minds. Freddie, their oldest child, was now fully recovered after a dangerous few months in hospital.

A tumour, benign but against a part of the brain that caused the surgeon anxiety, had to be removed. Freddie's condition, before and after the operation, veered between safe and terrifyingly unstable, for an interminable three days.

The Three
Wise Men
are waiting,
Standing proudly
in the wings.
A pin is almost
heard to drop,
And then the
choir sings!

Right on cue the angels come
To bless the little scene.
The shepherds' faces all aglow —
They've never looked so clean!

When all the cast go home at last,
Each ready for some sleep,
The only one not tired
Is a threadbare little sheep!

— *Sandra Robinson.*

His road to recovery had been slow and exhausting, and they had two much younger children to look after as well.

Neil knew that his wife had been changed for ever by the experience. She watched her children's health very closely, although she tried to pretend she didn't.

"Freddie's the healthiest ten-year-old I've ever seen," Neil said.

"I know, I know. I'm an idiot."

"You said it. About a minute ago, I think," he replied.

"But you take my point. When you have a handsome, kind husband, with a reasonably secure job —" his laugh interrupted her momentarily "— and the three most precious children imaginable, it can make you wonder if life is too . . . charmed. It hangs on a thread, Neil." She paused. "I'm happy, you see."

"Only you could make that sound like a problem."

Sian ignored him.

"You know when you look at them all fast asleep?"

"I do. My wife pulls me into their rooms every blessed night so I can look at their angelic faces."

"Doesn't it make your heart miss a beat sometimes?"

"Yes, it does." He held her hand in the centre of the table. "They are all I've ever wanted, apart from you."

She twirled the damp leaf between her thumb and finger.

"Tansy wanted the ice store to stay exactly the same as when she found it. The frozen leaf made her so happy. She'll be devastated. She doesn't understand these things yet."

"She's not the only one. Look, my love, it's good to grab happiness when it's here. It's not so good to worry about it vanishing. I intend to make sure it never does. And we don't have time for worrying — we have this busy life. Normally."

Sian looked up, blinking as though woken from a dream.

"I don't often have time for thinking," she said.

"That's probably a good thing. And, anyway, I think your time just ran out." They could both hear the tumult approaching their front door.

T HE noise that burst in was equalled in intensity by the oncoming wave of hats, scarves and small bodies.

"Were they good?" Neil's voice rose above the chaos.

"Of course." Sian's sister dropped armfuls of bags on the hall floor.

"Sian, Ruby's got a paper cut. Don't believe her when she says it was her brother."

"Mummy, have you got my —"

"It's on the kitchen table, Tansy," Sian said, glancing at her husband.

They stayed in the hall, trying to get children separated from boots and wet coats, talking over each other. Tansy ran back from the kitchen.

"It's not there," she said. "Only a leaf or something. I left my bear in there and he's gone. He said he'd miss me so much that I had to bring him a present." She hurried up the stairs on a hunt for a soft toy.

"So, Tansy is distraught," Neil said to Sian, "about the melting of the ice store?" He kissed Ruby as she showed him her sticking plaster.

"I wonder if, actually, Tansy doesn't bother too much with dead stuff." He nearly toppled over as Freddie crashed into him.

"Freddie, have mercy," his aunt said. She strode past into the kitchen.

"Kettle on?"

"Fred, could you go up and see if Tansy's found that bear?" Neil said. He kneeled and faced his son.

"Hang on, you've got your jumper on back to front." He began to pull off the offending article of clothing.

"We have three things here, Sian, that are very much alive, and no time to worry about what might not happen tomorrow." He looked up. "Sian?"

But she had gone, dragged by Tansy into the living-room. The little girl was telling her mother about the "really cool" girl she'd met in the park with Auntie Betty. He heard Sian's bright laugh through the door.

"She's happy, your mum," he said to Freddie.

"Great," he replied. "What's for tea?" ■